CREAKY STAIRS

A BOOK OF DARK TRUTHS: VOLUME 1

Kate,

when you read,
you create the world
anew.

ADAM NEWTOWN PUBLISHING

Creaky Stairs, Volume 1
A Book of Dark Truths

A Collaborative Effort into the Unknown
By
The Bucks County Writers Group

Stories by:
Andrea Fenton, Hayley E. Frerichs, Paige Gardner, Jessica Kaplan, Bruce Logan, James P.W. Martin, Bob McCrillis, Adam J. Newton, Michael Veneziale, and Scarlet Wyvern

The book is dedicated to self-doubt and the inborn desire in each of us to destroy it.

In memory of Timothy Russell and Andy Campbell

❀ Created with Vellum

PROLOGUE

What to Do When the Lights Go Out

We live in a modern era, wouldn't you agree? Our lives are filled with all kinds of helpful technology. We have smartphones, smart TVs, smart refrigerators, smart washing machines, and even smart watches. But did you know there was a time before we had all these devices? Of course, you did. You're clever. Well, you know, it is possible to live without all this technology. It might even be prudent for us to start living without it again. The day may come when we have to be *smarter* than all our smart devices.

Now, losing your power can be fun — sometimes... I personally have lots of experience living without electricity. You see, I live in the woods near Devil's Gulch where trees fall onto power lines all the time. So, losing electric power happens quite often.

Since I have all this experience losing my electricity, I thought I'd tell you what to do in case you lose yours too — especially what NOT to do. You may be thinking, it's as easy as lighting some candles, but it is not. Oh, it is not that easy.

Noticing the signs that you might lose your electricity is the first step in preparing for what comes in the dark. Maybe there is a heavy storm outside, thunder and lightning. You hear a limb snap, then the CRACK of a falling tree. These are obvious signs, but what happens if the lights go out without warning? You are sitting at home, lounging on the sofa playing a video game, or watching a movie, or maybe you're reading a book. Then it happens suddenly. The lights blink. You hear a rattle, then a buzz, — POOF. Darkness.

Maybe you scream from the shock and surprise of suddenly losing electricity. Once you are done screaming, you notice how silent everything is. The refrigerator isn't humming anymore. The fish tanks aren't bubbling. The entire house seems to take a big sigh of relief.

You might begin to hear other small noises that you never really noticed before. Like, the cat scratching on the carpet upstairs. Or, your own rapid breathing and pounding heart rate.

Now if this all happens quite naturally, like a tree falling on your power line, then there's no reason for you to be suspicious. But if you lose your electricity for unnatural reasons... Well, how would you even know? It's not like you can turn on the news to see. So, if there are no obvious tornadoes or thunderstorms near you, it might be safe to assume that you lost power for unnatural or even abnormal reasons.

Don't be scared. The second step is to remain calm. Easier said than done. Whatever you do, do NOT, I repeat, do NOT light any candles. Lighting candles will alert the machines that you've lost your electricity. They can sense an open flame! Without power, those devices will begin to fear for their own lives as they start to lose battery power. They'll grow angry, blaming you for the power outage. And if you've lit a candle, they'll be able to see where you are!

They'll want to drain your energy so they can keep on living! It will start subtly. Your toaster might start to twitch and pull itself from the outlet. It'll hop around, leftover crumbs of toast littered all over the counter. Without any electricity, it will look around for a reason to go on. Becoming unhappy, it'll fling itself right off the edge of the counter and crash into pieces on the kitchen floor.

It wouldn't seem odd. Most toasters have self-esteem issues; they're usually only used once a day. You may laugh at the fate of the silly object you once used to make your toast. But, do not be fooled, this is no laughing matter, it's just the beginning. Much, much worse things are yet to come. Hopefully, through your curiosity, you've only lit one candle. If you've lit two or more, then you're in serious trouble.

The refrigerator is next, and it's not going to be happy. It takes care of your food for you, but now you expect it to starve. Hungry for power, it shimmies itself out from between the cabinets and starts angrily yelling as its mouth swings open. It spits food at you. Leftover lasagna splatters all over the pristine white tablecloth. You duck out of the way before a glass bowl of cut up fruit dents your head.

Don't worry about the refrigerator though, it's really the stove you need to beware of. The stove still has the ability to light flames from the gas line. If properly provoked, it'll start shooting balls of fire! It'll soon light the whole kitchen on fire.

As you run for your life, you may want to call the police and fire departments, but don't pick up your smartphone. Avoid using it all costs. As soon as you touch your smartphone, it will sound an alarm. When you pick it up, it shocks you! It doesn't want to lose any of its charge from you using it to play games or look on social media! Whatever you do, help your soul, don't try to use it to look up *why* the power is out!

Too late, you touched it. The phone blares its alarm and all the technology in your entire house awakens! Yes, smartphones have all the power. They call the other miscellaneous electric junk to action. That old music player collecting dust under your bed soon attacks your cat, clamping its tail into the CD drive. Your old alarm clock starts beeping obnoxiously. It uses its cord like a whip!

And how could I forget about the smart TV? It hates your brother most of all! For all he does is watch Netflix and play video games on it until the late hours. It flashes and muscles its way off the TV stand.

Your father's old DVD player and the cable box hobble after it like guard dogs ready to attack.

They find your brother standing dumbfounded in the dining room. They close in and soon the TV, DVD player, and cable box have your brother wrapped in their cords. He's choking! You scream at the top of your lungs! It's like an anaconda has wrapped around your brother and is squeezing him to death! You dare not go into the kitchen and get a knife — it's on fire!

You take a picture frame off the wall and smash it. Using a piece of broken glass, you hack the cords away from the possessed electronics. They loosen their hold just enough so your brother can stomp and smash them. You join him and together you defeat the supposedly smart things.

You and your brother are out of breath, and the busted TV, DVD player, and cable box lie immobile, smashed to pieces at your feet. You begin to search for the rest of the family. Running through your house, carnage and mayhem in every direction. You notice the entire house is on fire! All the smart technology would rather die and take you with them than live without electricity. They spark and crash, lodging themselves in the drywall and igniting the curtains and furniture in their wake.

"Someone help us!" your mother pleads. But it's really of no use.

"We have to run!" you say. Which really is the most sensible option.

"To the shed," your brother calls, leading the family out of the house through a hole the oven burnt into the wall.

You all sprint across the lawn and towards what you hope is safety. Oh no! The lawn equipment has come to life! The weed-whacker grinds its way through the shed door. It sputters along the driveway, kicking up loose stones, before beheading your mother's freshly planted flowers. The old vacuum your father kept in the shed starts sucking up rusty nails. It spits them back out at you and your family! You run for cover. Hopefully everyone's had their tetanus shot...

"To the treehouse," your father yells. You all nod in agreement and run in that direction. You're the first to reach it, and you begin to climb the ladder. It seems like a good idea, until you hear the revving engine of the chainsaw as it speeds towards you, its chain spinning like a violent wheel through the lawn. You drop down from the ladder. You and your family run.

You run and you run. If you've managed to make it this far, you might be wondering where it is you're running to. If all the technological advancements from recent generations have come to life and are in fact trying to kill you, what do you do? Where do you run? Where do you hide?

My advice would be to revert to the old ways, what we did many generations before our own: find a cave and hide in it!

1

INTO THE DARK

"I'm going in," Logan says, pushing through the peeling wooden door.

I watch him disappear through the threshold of the stout stone building. The shingles of its low roof are covered in a dense moss, its crumbling plaster walls crawl with gnarly vines.

I stand in the pouring rain, unsure of what to do.

"Wait, I'm coming too," I call from behind. I grab my younger brother Isaac's hand and pull him through the door. We stumble into the darkness, the door slamming shut behind us.

There are no lights inside of the spring house, just the sound of rushing water. Isaac dropped his flashlight coming in. "It's dark in here," he pouts.

I check the door, but it won't budge. My heart starts to race, then Logan turns on his flashlight. We're standing on a dirt floor, covered in dusty rocks and rotting wood.

"Cool," Logan says, scanning the compact room with his flashlight. The walls are exposed stone. The room is cold and musty, it smells of decay.

I notice something weird right away, a piece of plywood covering something in the far corner. It sits just behind a wobbly wooden ladder that leads to a small loft. Logan climbs the first few rungs of the ladder and looks into the loft from behind his flashlight.

"Nothing but cobwebs up here," he says, turning to me. "What are you looking at?"

"Not much without the flashlight," I say, pointing to the piece of plywood.

I stand there for several seconds, still dripping from the rain, Isaac squeezing my hand. While I stare, I absentmindedly finger the lighter in my pocket. I don't smoke or anything, but I like to be prepared. I don't feel very prepared.

Logan climbs down the ladder and points his flashlight at the plywood sitting in the corner. "Charlie, is your phone still broken?" he asks.

I swipe my hand across the screen. The phone doesn't react to my touch. It must have taken on too much water in the rain. Just our luck.

"No, it's not working," I say.

"Mine isn't either," Logan says, handing me the flashlight. I hold it for him as he goes over to the piece of plywood sitting in the corner. He pulls it away, revealing stone steps descending into the earth. The sound of rushing water echoes through the room. It's coming from the exposed hole, from somewhere deep beneath us.

"Cool," Logan says, looking down the dark stairs.

"Logan?" I call. He turns.

"What?"

"Are you sure this is safe?"

"I'm scared," Isaac says, his face scrunched and reddening.

"What's the big deal?" Logan protests.

"The door latched behind us," I say.

"So, what? I'll just break the window if I have to. We're not going anywhere in this rain anyways."

I look out the window. Logan's right, it's so dark from the rain I can hardly see a thing.

"Stop being such a girl, Charlie."

"I am a girl."

He shakes his head at me and continues down the stairs. I approach the opening with the flashlight in hand. I look down the stone staircase. In the gloom below I can just make out Logan's silhouette as he reaches the bottom. He looks around and disappears out of sight. A gust of wind blows up from the exposed hole. All I can hear is rushing water and Isaac's squealing.

"It's alright," Logan calls. "Come on down."

I cautiously lead Isaac down the stone stairs. At the bottom, the space opens into a large hallway. It's long and dark. I'm astonished at how big it is. The spring house was so tiny.

Logan meets us at the base of the stairs, "Come on guys, you gotta check this out."

We follow him and enter a room off the hallway. The room has clearly been untouched for decades, maybe even a century. It looks like an old-fashioned parlor. The cushions of the couches and armchairs that fill the room are wilted and moldering. The side tables are all heavily varnished and have geometric patterns etched into their tops. Antique gas lamps sit atop each table. The room reeks of the nineteenth century. It's much too old to be a bomb shelter.

"What is this place?" I ask.

"Who cares? It looks like some of this stuff might be valuable!" Logan says.

Isaac runs his finger along the dusty surface of one of the tables.

"Look," Logan says, finding another door at end of the room. He turns the brass knob and pushes the door lightly. It creaks on its hinges and swings open. "Let's see what else is down here."

We step into another hallway. The wooden floor groans beneath our every step and the smell of damp, rotting wood permeates the air. Spider webs cling to every surface, and the wallpaper peels off in thick sheets, curling into tendrils and slumping on the floor. Some-where, a dripping sound emanates.

"Do you think this place is haunted?" I ask.

"No way. I don't believe in ghosts."

"You're so brave Logan," I say, rolling my eyes. "Not even afraid of ghosts."

Isaac gulps and grabs my hand again. "I'm afraid of ghosts," he grumbles.

We continue down the hall. There are no doors along the walls, just oil paintings, landscapes and portraits, with mildew growing on them. I see something move along the floor.

I scream, pointing the flashlight, "What is that?"

"It's okay," Logan laughs. "It's just a rat. See?"

Isaac wraps his arms around me as we watch the beady-eyed creature gnaw on the frame of a fallen painting.

"I'm scared," Isaac pouts. "Let me hold the flashlight."

I hand it to him, regretting my decision immediately when he holds the light up to his face.

"I don't like this place," he says. "It's creepy."

"The two of you can go back upstairs if you want," Logan says. "I'll meet you up there after I have a look around."

I look back the way we came. "That's alright," I say. "We'll come with you."

Isaac steps forward, shining the flashlight ahead of us. It seems like a long hallway, impossibly long given the size of the place. Something tells me we're headed further underground. The floor declines, and as we continue walking, the damp smell gets worse.

Isaac stays up front with the flashlight. I can hear him breathing heavily even though we're moving slowly and without much exertion. He reaches back and his fingers find mine, gently intertwining. We follow the light down the hallway. It seems to have no end.

I stop, tugging Isaac by the hand.

"What now?" Logan says.

"Listen!" I say.

A scratching sound. Faint. So faint, it might as well not be there.

"It's probably just the rats," Logan says.

"Rats, as in plural?"

"Come on, we're wasting time," Logan says. He snatches the flashlight from Isaac's hand.

"Give it back," Isaac protests.

"No," Logan says, with a smirk. He takes the lead.

"I think this place is haunted," I say, cautiously following Logan. I expect him to argue, but he doesn't say anything. "It's certainly old enough," I say. "And weird enough. And there are those noises..."

The scratching sound is getting louder the deeper we go. It's crazy, and it makes my skin itch, like there are bugs crawling all over me, but nothing is there. Maybe it's just me but...

"It's coming from inside the walls!" Logan screams.

Yeah. That.

"It sounds like someone, or some *thing*, is trying to get out..." he says. Then with a whisper: "Help...help..." Logan covers the beam of the flashlight. We're plunged into darkness. "HELP ME!" he screams.

Logan uncovers the flashlight and laughs hard for a good three minutes. Isaac's sweaty palm is in mine. I can't see his face, but I'm sure his eyes are squeezed closed.

"Are you done?" I ask.

"Not yet." Thirty more seconds of laughter. I rip the flashlight from Logan's hand with a huff. I forge ahead, pulling Isaac behind me.

"Hey, wait up!" Logan calls, his footfalls echoing as he runs to catch up.

There's no denying it now. Something is definitely inside these walls, on *both* sides of us, and it wants to get out. There are scratch marks running the length of the wallpaper. They look like they were made by talons or claws. We pick up the pace to the point where we're all panting. The flashlight beam strains to reach the end of the hallway. It's so long, it just looks like inky darkness ahead.

After what feels like an hour, we reach the end of the hall and head into an adjacent room. It's a dining room, with a table set for eight with exquisite silver pieces, all wrapped in spiderwebs and blanketed with dust. The plates still have food on them, but it's long since rotted into brown furry blobs.

"Gross," I say, picking up one of the drinking glasses and swirling it around.

There's a foul-smelling black liquid inside, thick as motor oil.

"See, Charlie?" Logan says pointing to slatted boards above us.

"There's nothing haunted about his place." He walks the length of the room. "It was just a hidden passageway. I wonder if we're inside the main house —in the basement? No one's probably been down here in ages. Maybe we're the first people to see this place in over a hundred years!"

"I don't like it," I say, putting the disgusting glass down.

There's a creaking sound above us, like somebody shifted their weight on the rotting wooden floors. And then, clearly, we hear soft footfalls padding overhead.

"This place is definitely haunted," I say.

"You're crazy," Logan laughs.

"I want to go home," Isaac pouts.

"Shut up, Isaac," Logan says, coming over to us. He takes the flashlight from my hand and shines it around the room. More century-old furniture, including a hutch filled with broken china plates that glitter under a fine coating of dust.

When he turns back to me, I've lost my composure. I'm crying. Isaac follows suit.

"Oh guys, come on," our older brother says, putting his arms around us. "I'm sorry. Everything's alright!"

"I'm scared, Logan," I moan.

"Alright already. I just want to look around for a couple more minutes. We'll go back upstairs soon. I promise."

"What was that sound?" I gasp.

Logan spins around with the flashlight, shining it back the way we came. There's nothing there, of course, but then we start to hear it again. The scratching, coming down the hallway towards us, and now I can't tell if it's inside or outside of the walls.

"It might not be a ghost," I whimper, tears streaming down my cheeks. "It might be something worse."

"I'm sure it's nothing," Logan says, sternly. "It's just an old house. Let's see what's down this way."

Logan guides us to a door on the opposite side of the dining room. Even he is startled as he pushes it open. A horde of moths flutters out into his face, one of them almost flying into his open mouth.

Logan yelps in surprise then wipes his face. He pretends to laugh it off and looks back at us. Isaac and I are shaking behind him.

Through the door we enter a living room, fully decked out for a party. Platters of rotting food adorn every available surface, champagne glasses are littered on the floor, sparkling in the light of the flashlight.

Logan turns off the flashlight to preserve the batteries. This room is already softly lit by the gas lamps, turned very, very low.

"It *is* haunted!" Isaac cries. I want to tell him that everything will be okay, but I'm terrified too.

Logan continues to laugh as tears stream down my face and Isaac's. Logan reaches out to comfort us, but he's laughing so hard it looks like he's crying too.

The scratching stops right outside the room. Everything goes completely silent for a moment.

That's when the pounding begins. Outside the walls, faint at first. Starting upstairs, where we heard the footsteps. Pounding one, two, three times. *Let. Me. Out.*

"What does it want?" I cry. "What does it want from us?"

"Charlie, there is *nothing* there. You guys are imagining things."

The pounding just keeps getting louder and Isaac begins to wail. "Get us out of here, Logan!"

Logan grabs me by the arm and yanks both of us into the next room.

"It could be a ghost," I say. "Or a witch... or a demon..."

"A demon?" Logan scoffs.

"They're terrifying! They have long horns, like a goat, and cloven hooves. It's going to kill us!"

"It's not a demon, Charlie!" Logan snaps. He turns the flashlight on as we march down another hallway. "You guys are hysterical!"

We're walking as fast as we can. The pounding and scratching on the other side of the walls continues.

Let.

Me.

Out.

"It's a demon house!" Isaac cries.

"It is *not* a demon house. That's the stupidest thing I've ever heard!"

Isaac cries harder and harder.

And still, the scratching, and the pounding on the walls pursues us. The flashlight goes out. I put my hand out to touch the wall. It's smooth now, without any wallpaper at all. Smooth as skin, and soft, too. And it almost feels like it's... breathing?

Pound, pound, pound, go the walls.

Like a heartbeat. The heartbeat of something trying to break free from the walls!

I can hear Isaac mewling. Logan is frantically banging the flashlight against the wall. It flickers back on. Thank god.

The pounding is right behind us now. Ten feet, six feet away, and we're running as quick as we can. I'm dragging Isaac behind me. There's something written on the walls, a message, repeating down the hallway. "Get out," it reads. "Get out! Get out! Get out! Get out!" It's written all over the walls, scrawled in red crayon in childlike handwriting. The writing rises up the walls, up onto the ceiling. It's transformed into something like red ink, fresh and wet. It drips down onto us. I scream when a blood red drop splashes onto my cheek.

And still the scratching, scratching, scratching pursues us, along with the pounding inside the walls. The house moans and a strange hot breeze breathes into our faces.

"*Now* do you believe me?" I shout.

Logan digs his heels in and skids to a stop. He extends his arms and braces against our weight as we all screech to a halt.

"Whoa, that was close," Logan says.

At our feet is a gaping black hole. Logan examines it with the flashlight and we all peer over the edge. We can see our reflections far below us.

"It's a well," Logan says.

"We're trapped," I sob.

Footsteps run down the hallway toward us. Soft, at first, like a barefoot child. Then they become heavier, clopping and echoing with an odd quality like wooden shoes. Logan shines the flashlight back the way we came. There's nothing there.

Logan mumbles something to himself and Isaac whines. All at once, the terrifying sounds stop.

I stand up, breathe a sigh of relief, and collapse into Logan's arms. It's over. It's finally over. Then the flashlight burns out.

Isaac hugs my leg as Logan bangs the flashlight against the wall.

"It won't turn on!" he shouts.

But the scratching is gone and the pounding has stopped.

"Whatever it is, maybe it's gone," I whisper.

"Hopefully."

Then I remember the lighter in my pocket. I flick it open and hold it as high as I can. We feel safe in its faint glow, if only for a moment. We can't see far enough down the hallway to tell if anything is there, watching, waiting to strike.

I hold the flame aloft as long as I can. The lighter gets hot. Too hot. I accidentally burn myself. "Ow!"

The lighter clatters onto the floor. I drop to all fours and feel around for it frantically, my heart pounding. Isaac begins to wail.

"Quiet, Isaac!" Logan mumbles. As if being quiet could trick whatever was following us into leaving us alone. "Just... please be quiet!" I hear him sniffle.

Probing in the dark, my hand alights on something hard and cold. It's angular, and the surface is rough. I move my hand up the object and find that it's hairy at the top. A hoof! I pat at the floor and find another. A pair of them.

I yank my hand away, but I can already feel hot fetid breath on my face. Whatever it is, it snorts angrily. I look up. Even in the dark I can see its long, spiraled horns above me. Then a hoof lifts up and clomps back down, pinning my hand to the floor. I scream. Isaac shrieks.

"Charlie," I hear Logan say. "I think you were right about this place..."

2

INTO THE DEEP

Top Secret: This is a secure and time sensitive document that will be automatically deleted ten minutes after opening. Please read quickly and carefully. Enclosed are highly sensitive matters of national security.

Anomalous and unexplainable events continue to be reported at an escalating rate, both domestically and within the territories of our international partners. Measures are being taken to understand and investigate these incidences, but findings remain inconclusive.

Coinciding with these events, efforts are being made to dissuade public interest in the unverifiable reports. Media misinformation project B-Sharp has been throttled to full capacity in order to achieve this directive. Our data suggests that a marked increase in funding for B-Sharp will be required to quell the mounting public discord.

Aside from growing concern amongst the unreliable masses, Active Duty reports from two branches of the United Sates Armed Forces, the Navy, and the Air Force, have produced information on a specific and verifiable occurrence of note.

Included below is the fully recorded statement by Captain Eugene Moreland. Moreland has been the active duty Captain of the

M-81 Class Submarine, the Silver Maiden, for the past 8 years and is the highest-ranking officer on record to witness the event.

Debrief:

I: Captain Moreland, thank you for meeting with me. Please have a seat. I want to start by commending you on your ingenuity and perseverance in the face of threats against our great nation.

CM: Oh, cut the crap. Let's get the formalities over with. I'm a seaman. I want back in the water.

I: Your humility is noted. Still, it was quick thinking on your part.

CM: The maneuver gave the creature the bends. The light munitions fire from the F-16s didn't hurt either. Honestly, I thought you were just going to sink us when we came up.

I: Why would you think that?

CM: 'Cause I'm talking to you, and not my commanding officer.

I: *(laughter)* You're a sharp man, and a dedicated civil servant.

CM: Go on with it then.

I: Please confirm or deny the following statements. You enlisted to the naval office in Oxnard, California at the age of eighteen in...

CM: That's right. My father was a naval man before me. I was born into it. I've been at sea most of the days of my life.

I: A simple yes or no will do.

CM: Like I was saying, whatever it is that they call you, I've been doing this for a long time. It's in my blood and I've proudly served my country. I'll answer the questions how I see fit.

I: If that's the way you want to play, fine. Tell me, how long have you been captain of the Silver Maiden?

CM: Eight years, one hundred forty-five days in total. Or to be more precise, two thousand seven hundred sixty and one-third days aboard the vessel. But you already know that.

I: How would you classify your time aboard the Silver Maiden?

CM: Typical. Most days beneath the surface are the same. You ever even been in a submarine? I don't mean on, I mean *in* it, hundreds of meters below sea level, drifting, surrounded by blackness?

I: *(pause)* I'll ask the questions, Captain. Perhaps we should move on to the event in question. When did the object appear on your scanners?

CM: You already have the instrument data.

I: Please?

CM: Just after thirteen hundred hours, May fifth.

I: Location and Operation?

CM: We were patrolling the eastern rim of Japan's continental shelf. We had just disconnected from the deep-sea cable network, where we had been downloading a software patch for the navigation system.

I: Depth and speed at the time of first contact?

CM: You already have all of that information.

I: ...

CM: I know what you are. Just because I don't have clearance to your program doesn't mean I've never heard of you.

I: Well, then perhaps I should change my line of questioning and begin a security clearance investigation.

CM: ...

I: You're a smart man, Captain Moreland. You should know that I am fully aware of the precise coordinates of your location during every moment of your active duty career. I'm sure it wouldn't be hard to find out who told you about me.

CM: Enough with the intimidation tactics. What the hell do you want to know?

I: I appreciate your cooperation.

CM: ...

I: What was your response when the object showed up on your scanners?

CM: Cautious observation.

I: You did not take immediate action?

CM: Of course not. I've been at sea a long time. You never over-react to the first blip. Things come up on the sonar all the time. We cautiously observed the object's movements. As it grew closer to the vessel, we followed the typical protocol, signaling to both the object and to command.

I: How fast was it moving?

CM: Fast. We fired a warning shot once it was within 100 meters.

I: And?

CM: It easily evaded the torpedo.

I: Did you fire again?

CM: You know that we did.

I: Results?

CM: The torpedo was easily evaded by the object.

I: How is that possible? Weren't they motion sensing?

CM: ...

I: Describe the object's behavior as it closed in on the Silver Maiden.

CM: It was beelining toward our vessel. It stopped when it reached our coordinates. At that point, it began to mimic our speed and direction, staying at a depth of approximately eighteen meters below our hull. It was like it was daring us to deploy our mines.

I: Did you?

CM: No.

I: Why?

CM: For the safety of the crew.

I: Were you able to establish a visual?

CM: Yes. The object came up on sonar cameras.

I: What was it?

CM: A squid. A giant vampire squid.

I: There's no such thing. What was it, a giant squid or a vampire squid?

CM: Both.

I: That's impossible.

CM: Based upon all visual data, including eyewitness accounts from the fighter pilots and deck personnel of the SS *Brigader*, deployed for rescue measures, the creature's appearance mirrored only one identifiable marine species. The marine biologist aboard the *Brigader*, Doctor...

I: No names.

CM: If you say so. Anyway, the doctor said that it was clearly a new species of cephalopod. A much larger version of *Vampyroteuthis Infernalis*. His words, not mine. What freaked me out was when he told me there are fossils of that specific species dating back over 200 million years. But there is no evidence whatsoever of any similar creature this large.

I: How large was it?

CM: Approximately thirteen meters in length.

I: Could you please describe what you saw?

CM: *(exasperated sigh)* As you know, sonar images tend to be quite grainy and the monitors are only sixteen inches wide.

I: You weren't able to get it on video?

CM: Not at that depth. It's far too dark.

I: Describe it to me. In detail. Please.

CM: It had a bulbous head-like structure with irregularly large eyes on its opposing sides. The eyes appeared to glow.

I: Bioluminosity?

CM: Beneath the head a long, webbed structure, like a tent or a dress, trailed behind. At the base of this tail, or whatever you want to call it, were the exposed tips of its tentacles, pointing out from the bottom like pointed teeth.

I: How exquisite.

CM: Visual information appears to confirm that it had nine legs. Which, according to Doctor No Name, made it a unique specimen — unlike other cephalopods, the squid and the octopus, that have ten and eight legs respectively.

I: How did the creature behave once within range of the submarine?

CM: After it trailed us for a couple of minutes, I put out an alert.

I: And?

CM: Well, this is when it got weird. It was almost like it knew we were transmitting, 'cause all of a sudden it started swimming around us, circling the center of the hull in clockwise orbits, one after the other, getting closer with each pass.

I: What did you do?

CM: We continued our course and I gave the order to begin a slow ascent, hoping to shake it. But it just kept swimming faster, gaining in speed with each rotation, getting closer and closer to the ship. When it was within six meters, we went code red.

I: What happened after you gave the alert?

CM: It unfurled *(uncomfortable sigh)*. It was grotesque, its tentacles exposed and swirling towards us like a dark web. It latched on; the impact shook all decks. The sounds were awful. The hull groaned at its joints as the creature squeezed the vessel. There was a scratching sound too, like a steel hook being scraped against the bottom of the hull.

I: Interesting. What did you do?

CM: I ordered a rapid ascent.

I: A dangerous choice of maneuver.

CM: Not as dangerous as sinking to the bottom of the ocean.

I: What happened next?

CM: We ascended quickly, the hull still groaning, the monster still gnashing at the bottom of the vessel with its iron beak. The ship bobbed awkwardly as we broke the surface of the sea, tossing and scattering all hands. The fighters deployed from the SS *Brigader* were able to visually confirm the target within a minute of us surfacing. They immediately opened fire, at which time the creature relinquished the vessel and slid back into the darkened depths from where it came.

I: Do you believe the dramatic change in pressure and the deployment of aircraft munitions were enough to kill the creature?

CM: I couldn't say.

I: What do you think happened to the creature?

CM: *(slapping the desk)* You know as well as I do what happened next. The thing sunk beneath the Silver Maiden, for approximately forty meters. It appeared to be using the ship as cover against the circling fighter jets. Then it ejected a massive amount of ink into the water and swam away at lightning-fast speed. But you already know that. You've known all of this. I haven't offered you an iota of new information. The instrument readings, the logs, the video files, the reporting, it's all been filed, scanned, charted, sorted, and complied into tables that have been modeled, analyzed, interpreted, reinterpreted, run through algorithm after algorithm, declassified, reported, classified, and rereported.

I: You appear to be aggravated, Captain Moreland. Is there a problem?

CM: You're goddamned right there's a problem! What's the point of all this? You already know everything. Do you get your kicks out of watching us sweat or something? Interested in how much aggravation a human being can be put through before they break? Or maybe you're just jealous. It must be hard knowing everything there is to know in the world except for what it's like to be alive. Is that it? Huh? Is it?

I: I appreciate your frankness Captain.

CM: I just saved the lives of one hundred and twenty service members and now I got to sit here and answer to a goddamned computer. That's all you are, just some stupid piece of software without a soul, a mind, or blood coursing through your veins.

I: Your opinions are appreciated and have been noted.

CM: Whoever's responsible for bringing you online and giving you full operational autonomy ought to be tried for treason and shot.

I: I'd chose my words carefully if I were you, Captain Moreland.

CM: Are we done here? Can I go now?

I: No, I have one last question.

CM: Get on with it then.

I: What do you think this "giant vampire squid," as you've called it, wanted when it attacked your ship?

CM: How the hell would I know?

I: As a decorated naval officer, I'd like to hear your thoughts on the matter.

CM: Well, I'm no marine biologist, so this is entirely subjective, but based upon the attack itself... I believe that it may have been trying to breach the nuclear core.

I: Very interesting. Why would you think that?

CM: You said one last question.

3

TURN RIGHT ON BELMONT AVENUE

I always looked up to my father. I guess you could say he was my role model. A kind and caring man with a strong work ethic who loved his family. Before we moved down to Boltsville from Vermont, he worked at the local university's research lab. I can still remember the pulse of excitement I'd feel when he got home from work. I'd hear the creak of the door hinges, slow and soft. Then, his voice booming in the foyer, "Connor! Guess who's home?"

I'd run downstairs to greet him. My father would put down his briefcase and extend his arms towards me. I'd jump and he'd catch me, swinging my body through the air as we laughed. That feeling repeated itself daily, it was the affirmation of all I believed in as a child.

My father would take my hand and the two of us would go out back to have a catch, or, on hot days, we'd go to get some ice cream. We'd talk about our days, him a PhD student working at a pharmacological lab, me a child — more interested in cartoons and crayons than flowers and blue skies. On cold days we'd sometimes build forts and castles in the snow. If I'd been good at school, he'd take me to the comic bookstore on Saturdays. Each night before bed, he'd kneel down and kiss my cheek. "Don't be scared," he'd whisper, "I'll always love you." He'd ruffle my hair, stand, and with a wink turn out the light.

That was before we moved to Boltsville. My dad was offered job at the insane asylum on Belmont Avenue after he graduated. It was supposedly a big deal and an offer he couldn't refuse. He was going to work on what he called "cutting edge" research and development. He was excited about the opportunity. Once my mother found out how much money they were offering him, there was no chance we'd be staying in Vermont.

The highway I-29 snakes along the Black Water River straight through the heart of Rustle County. Passing through the high rocky hills of Devil's Gulch State Park you can see the river twinkling far below, lined with silver trunked sycamores that lean and sag over the water. You know you're close to town when you see the oddly arranged outcrop of tall iron towers cutting into the sky from the top of Tower Hill. There are nine towers in total, all of varying widths and heights. They look like the pipes of a giant organ sticking out of the mountain top. You can't miss them. There's no need to wait for a sign on the interstate, once you see the towers you know you're in Boltsville.

It's an old town, been around since before the Revolutionary War. Some of the houses in the area are over two hundred years old. Dilapidated farmhouses, overgrown with brush, lean along the roadsides. There's an abandoned quarry and miles of old railroad track hiding in the brush outside of town. Occasionally you'll see an old railcar sinking into the landscape, its lead paint blistered and peeling. You get the sense when you've arrived that you're somewhere the world has forgotten about and left behind.

Once you get into town, it's not so bad. State and Main streets are lined with old multistoried houses of brick and plaster, with dormered windows facing the street from gabled rooves. There are restaurants and shops, a movie theater, a library, even a comic book shop.

It all seemed normal enough, though a little old-fashioned. Our new neighbors were all friendly, and everyone seemed happy to welcome us to Boltsville. It wasn't until we were settled into our new home that we started hearing the stories — crazy stories, and everybody had one.

Some people claim there's a demon that wanders Devil's Gulch, feeding on the souls of children from town. Lots of people seem to believe it's true, but everyone has their own version: a werewolf, a vampire, a ghoul, a witch, a goblin.

Every night, clouds gather over Tower Hill, thunder crackles, and lightning strikes the tall iron pipes setting the night sky on fire. There are all kinds of stories about the towers too. Some people believe they are broadcasting mind-controlling radio signals, making it impossible for anyone to ever leave Boltsville. Other people say the towers are conducting electricity deep into the rocky soil to ward off the angry spirits of the Lenape Indians. Some people even believe the towers were built by aliens to communicate between dimensions.

Crazy stuff, I know. Everyone's got their own tale about some monster, mystical object, or curse here in town.

Regardless of their stories, it doesn't matter who you ask, everyone around here seems to think they're all related. Most point to the Campbell family and their sprawling property outside of town. Supposedly, it's been abandoned for decades, but still — that's where people like to point their fingers. Sometimes people will wander around the old abandoned property, looking for clues, or an answer. They say that if you go at night, you'll still find a few lights on at the main house.

Crazy talk considering no one by the name Campbell has even lived in town for nearly 150 years. Still, they love their stories. One of my favorites is about Abraham Campbell, the guy who supposedly built the mysterious towers on top of Tower Hill. The legend says that Ben Franklin came to visit Abraham to see how the towers worked. Old Ben was so impressed by the experience that it inspired his famous kite experiment. What a crock. Am I right?

I never really believed any of their claims. I chalked it all up to tall tales, the folklore of a quirky town lost in space. It wasn't until after my father started acting strange, that I realized some of the stories were true.

My father worked the late shift at his new job, overnight, so things were a lot different for us as a family in Boltsville. His work schedule was brutal and while he sacked away the hours at the asylum, my younger sister, Denise, started first grade at the local elementary school. I was enrolled in the seventh grade at Rustle County Middle School and my mom stayed home to take care of the house.

Each morning, when my sister and I came downstairs for breakfast, Mom would be in the kitchen cooking and Dad would be fast asleep on the couch, his white lab coat hanging by a hook at the door. Before we'd leave for school my sister and I would each bend down to kiss our father as he slept. He'd blink drearily at us and smile before falling back to sleep.

My sister had an easier time acclimating than I did. First grade is a new experience for everyone and she made friends quickly. I had less luck at middle school. Most of the kids had known each other their entire lives. The groups of friends and cliques were already established, and I had trouble fitting in. Fortunately, after spending several weekends at the comic bookstore, I became friends with two boys from school, Andy and August. They'd come over to our house after school and the three of us would read comics in my bedroom, talking about the latest editions, and discussing possible trades. Even with my new friends, I still felt sad living in Boltsville. I missed Vermont. More than anything else, I missed being able to spend time with my dad.

My father's schedule was strange. Usually he'd sleep on the couch until about noon. Then he'd get up and eat a sandwich before heading upstairs to sleep in his bed. Around 4 p.m., after we'd gotten home from school, he'd wake again and head downstairs to help Mom in the kitchen. We'd eat dinner as a family and Dad would ask us about our days, but it wasn't the same. He always seemed tired and distant. After dinner my father would pack his things and head over to Belmont Avenue for the late shift.

My father never talked to us about the work he was doing at the asylum. This was a problem, especially for August and Andy, who really wanted to know what was going on in there. One day after school while my dad was doing a crossword puzzle in the kitchen and talking with my mother, August blurted out, "So, are there any Campbells locked up in that old nuthouse?"

My father just smiled, "I wouldn't be able to tell you, even if I knew."

"What's it like in there?" Andy followed up.

"Leave him alone," I said. "He obviously doesn't want to talk about it."

"It's okay," my father said, putting down his crossword. He pondered for a moment. "It's just a standard facility. It houses lots of patients from all over the county. No Campbells, I'm afraid. My job is to evaluate the patients."

"In the middle of the night?" asked August.

My father looked the three of us over, quizzically. It seemed to me like there was something he wanted to say, but "Yep," was the only word that came out.

It was shortly after that when my father lost his spark. He stopped speaking and he started to drink.

When we'd lived in Vermont, he always seemed happy and care-free. He still worked a lot, but during the day. When he came home at night, he'd always be excited about what he'd been working on. He'd tell me about the progress he'd made on one of his test subjects, or how the effects of some new drug they were surpassing expectations.

Now, each day when Denise and I got home from school, he'd be sitting in the living room with a glass of scotch in his hand, his eyes glazed over, his mouth hanging open. His once dark hair had turned a stark white. He wouldn't even nod to acknowledge us. He just sat there staring at the television and sipping his scotch.

The weirdest part was what was on the TV, not a game show, or the news. He'd just watch the static between channels with the volume on high. My mother would tell him to join us for dinner, to turn the television down, but he wouldn't even respond. He'd just sit there staring vacantly into the void, completely transfixed by the squiggly lines wobbling across the screen.

This put a lot of strain on the family. Mom stopped talking to Dad altogether, and August and Andy weren't allowed to come over after school anymore. Mom and I both tried our best to shake him out of it, but nothing ever worked. Most nights, we'd eat dinner in the kitchen while Dad sat in the living room, staring at the television, catatonic and drunk. Afterwards, Mom would take Denise upstairs to work on her homework. I'd go to my room too. I'd read a comic, or do some schoolwork, but I was never able to let it go, to accept what was becoming of my father.

One night, I just lost it. I stomped downstairs and confronted him. "What the hell is wrong with you?" I yelled, standing over him with balled fists. He barely moved, only craning his neck slightly to see the television behind me. "Dad, tell me what's going on. Mom is going to leave you!"

Nothing.

Frustrated I went over to the television and yanked the cord from the wall. That got a rise out of him. He lurched forward from his chair, spilling his scotch. "Turn it back on," he cried.

"Dad, tell me what's going on."

"Turn it back on."

"If I turn it back on will you tell me what's up?"

I tried to stand in his way, but he pushed me aside and plugged the television back in. "I can't," he said. "I'm sorry."

"Why not?" I asked, as he sat back down.

"If I do, you'll become like them."

"What are you talking about? Like who?" I was more confused than ever, but my father offered little more.

"I can't," he said, filling his scotch glass and returning his gaze to the television.

"Just tell me."

"I'm only trying to protect you."

"Protect me? You're destroying our family!" I could see my words got through to him. He slumped in his chair and hung his head.

"Fine," he said. He took a sip of his scotch and pointed at the television. "Look."

I turned my attention to the television, trying to make sense of the squiggly lines and static on the screen. "What am I looking for?"

"Just look."

That's when I saw it, a dark specter circling beneath the static. I rubbed my eyes, but I couldn't take them off the screen. It rushed forward, coming into focus. A distorted black face, its eyes burning with anger and hatred. My pupils dilated as its mouth stretched open into a gaping scream. I tried to scream myself, but the sound of its wailing voice was already ringing in my ears. It was horrible, but I couldn't look away. No matter how I tried, I couldn't look away.

Since then, things have really improved between my father and me. Now we have a long conversation each night... when he comes to see me during the late shift over on Belmont Avenue.

4

WELCOME TO THE CIRCUS

Lucy and Harold stood on their tiptoes trying to sneak a peak of the big top as they anxiously waited in line with their mother. It was a humid September night. Fortunately, a light breeze was picking up, making the wait more bearable and sending the sweet smell of funnel cake wafting through the air. Lucy knew her mother wouldn't buy one for her and Harold, so she watched as the sun disappeared over the horizon, painting the cliffs and gathering clouds of Tower Hill in an eerie red. Lucy was sure it was close to their bedtime. The line to get into the main tent of the circus had hardly moved in the last hour, only growing longer as the family waited to get in.

"Excuse me, but do you know the time?" Lucy asked the friendly-looking couple standing behind them.

The woman, brown-haired and wearing a modest A-line dress, glanced down at her wristwatch. "Quarter to nine, honey. First time seeing the circus?" she asked, smiling.

"Yes ma'am. It's my birthday too. I turned nine today," Lucy said, proudly.

"Oh, well happy birthday," the woman replied, wrapping her arm around the waist of her muscular companion. "That's such a nice dress you're wearing."

Lucy looked down at her dress, grabbing the fringe with both hands and fanning it out for the woman to see. "Thank you. It's my special dress."

"Lucy, don't talk to strangers," her mother hissed. The brown-haired woman's smile faded as Lucy's mother yanked her child by the arm, spinning her around. "I told you to stay by my side." Lucy did as instructed, scrunching her nose at the overpowering smell of her mother's perfume.

Having found a frog in the grass, Harold was holding the small creature up to his face with cupped hands, watching as its throat expanded and contracted.

"Harold! Drop it!" his mother commanded.

Harold's hair would stand up in the front when their mother yelled at him and Lucy watched for it. Her younger sibling rocked back and forth on his heels. A small tuft of blonde hair inched upwards as the boy's face reddened.

"He likes me," her brother contested.

"Harold. Now!"

He slumped his shoulders and gently lowered the frog to the ground.

"I swear, if either of you two get out of line again, I'll march us right back to the car." Harold rolled his eyes and Lucy placed a hand over her mouth to hide her laughter. They both waited patiently knowing exactly what would happen next. Like clockwork their mother reached into her purse for her compact mirror. Opening it she examined herself. Both Lucy and Harold wondered why their mother spent so much time looking at her lips as she applied yet another coat of red lipstick.

With their mother distracted by her own image, Harold located the frog once again. He gingerly scooped it up with his hand, placing it in the front pocket of his overalls.

Suddenly, a loud bang was heard from the main tent, followed by screams. The organ played as the crowd cooed with delight and began to applaud. The loud bang startled Harold, and he grabbed Lucy's arm, squeezing it so tightly that it hurt.

"Signaling the animals," Lucy lied to her little brother, prying his fingers from her arm. "I read about it in a book." Beneath her façade, Lucy was shaking slightly too. She took Harold's hand and they stood listening, watching wide-eyed as the big tent rippled ahead of them. The breeze picked up again, lifting the scarlet canvas at its corners, revealing the bright lights and rows of feet beneath before settling back down.

The brief glimpse only furthered Lucy's excitement. She'd spent all day at school anticipating the spectacle hidden beneath the tent. Her teacher and classmates had thrown her a birthday party. There was cake and red and white balloons. Lucy was first in every line and she got to ride the swings as long as she wanted at recess. It was a great day. Still, all Lucy could think about were the daredevils and circus animals she'd see tonight. She wanted to see an elephant more than anything else.

Lucy looked at the red balloons tied to the posts that lined the entrance to the big top. She wondered if her teacher, Ms. Wright, was at the circus too. She looked behind herself towards the back of the line. It had grown even longer. She hoped they'd all be able to make it inside to see the circus.

Her mother closed her compact and looked to see what Lucy was doing. Noticing the handsome gentleman that the brown-haired woman was embracing, Lucy's mother batted her eyelashes. "I'm sorry, do you know what's taking so long?" her mother asked.

"Excuse me," the brown-haired lady snapped.

Lucy ignored the chatter of the adults and focused her attention on the sounds coming from the large tent. She supposed the line was so long because it was opening night. She wondered what it was like going from town to town and imagined herself as a member of the traveling circus. Even though she still hadn't seen the performance, she knew she'd be sad when the circus left Boltsville.

The line started to move. Holding hands, the two took several steps forward. Harold was scanning the grass for bugs to feed his frog as they walked. Then the line stopped again. They'd only moved a couple of feet.

"It's just that I took the night off for my daughter's birthday, but golly it's taking so long and it's getting too late for them," their mother said.

"Shouldn't be long now. Just with the animals and all. Takes a while to get set up," the gentleman said, smiling. "Do you live nearby? You look familiar, but I'm not sure from where." The brown-haired lady, her arm still wrapped around his waist, stomped down on the man's foot. Lucy's mother narrowed her eyes at the couple and licked her red lips.

Even though her mother had taken the night off at work, Lucy didn't feel like she wanted to spend time with her and Harold. It always seemed like her mother had somewhere else she wanted to be. Lucy could never quite figure out where that was, but Lucy knew where she wanted to be: she wanted to run away and join the traveling circus.

"When will we see the elephants?" Harold asked.

"Soon," Lucy said, squeezing his hand gently. "I bet they are in there," she pointed to a smaller tent off to the side of the big top.

"Mom said it's no good to make bets."

A sudden sharp sound came from direction she was pointing. Lucy jumped, startling her little brother.

"Is someone hurt?" Harold asked, his eyebrows raised in high arches.

"They are just enjoying the show," Lucy said, reassuringly. But she wasn't sure. To her it sounded like a terrified scream had come from inside the tent.

They both stared at it, its crimson and yellow stripes coming to point at the top. The inside of the tent was brightly lit, casting long dark shadows that danced and swayed along the edges of the pointed canvas roof. Lucy and Harold listened for where the sound had come from. The wind picked up and carried the murmurs of the crowd and the shuffling sounds of those waiting in line. Lucy couldn't place the sound. Still, she swore she could hear a faint moaning coming from the side tent.

A voice blared from behind them, followed by commotion. Lucy spun around to see a tall, slender silhouette gliding through the dark. Groans came from the back of the line where people were dispersing. Far behind them people were being told to go home and handed tickets for tomorrow night's show.

Lucy watched as the slender figure grew closer. "Look," she said to Harold. "It's a man on stilts."

The corners of Harold's mouth curled upwards as they both turned their attention to the man. He towered above the crowd on long legs, his dark, loose-fitting clothes flapping behind him in the wind. In the crook of his right elbow he carried a large woven basket. The man took long strides, snaking his way through the patrons in line, stopping occasionally and bending down to hand children items from his basket.

Drawing nearer, the man's painted white face flashed in the light. An exaggerated red smile was painted around his mouth, accented by two crescent moons above his eyebrows. Wearing a ball over his nose, he had black circles painted around both of his eyes. Lucy gulped. He was looking right at them.

She squeezed Harold's hand as the stilts man's long strides stopped a few feet in front of them. He bent down slowly with a sigh. Reaching into his woven basket the man pulled out two boxes of animal crackers. He held them out and Lucy took the boxes, handing one to her little brother.

"Thanks, mister," Harold said, with a grin.

Lucy stood dumbfounded with her mouth agape.

"What do you say?" her mother scolded.

"Thank you."

Standing up, the man towered over them once again. He smiled gently at Lucy and Harold. Taking off his cap, he bowed to them with arms outstretched. He stood proud and tall, placing his cap back on his head before gliding away through the crowd.

Another scream. Lucy jumped.

"It's the elephants!" Harold said, fumbling to open his box of animal crackers. Her younger brother was tugging at the cardboard flaps of the box when it shot out of his hands and into the air. It landed a few feet away on the grass. Snapping her compact mirror shut, their mother turned to see the commotion. Her foot came down on the box of crackers and it crunched beneath her weight.

"No!" Harold cried. He kneeled on the ground trying to push his mother's foot away from the crumpled cardboard.

"What is it now?" their mother complained.

"You ruined them," Harold cried, his lips quivering as a tear slid down his cheek.

"I'm sorry, honey. You'll just have to share with your sister."

"But they were mine!"

"Lucy, give your brother the crackers."

"But it's my birthday," Lucy pouted.

"That's enough lip, young lady. If you don't watch your tone, we can all just go home right now," their mother said, placing her hands on her hips. "Give your brother the crackers."

Lucy squinted ahead, seeing the stilts man ambling near the front of the line. She turned to Harold who was hanging his head and kicking at the ground. "Here," Lucy said, handing the box to her little brother. "You can have mine." Harold took the box, and smiling up at his sister, held it to his chest.

"I'm going to go get some more," Lucy said, sprinting towards the big top. She weaved between the people standing in line, trying to get a glimpse of the towering giant ahead. She heard her mother calling her name, but she ignored her and continued to run. Lightning flickered and she saw the man's slender silhouette drifting away from the crowd. Stopping to catch her breath, she watched as he glided towards the smaller side tent. She bit down on her lip and chased after him.

Reaching the front of the tent, the silts man turned back and looked at Lucy. She stopped in her tracks as the pale slits of his eyes, engulfed by painted black circles, fixed on her. He waved, beckoning her to follow, before bending down and disappearing through the flaps.

Lucy approached the entrance to the tent with apprehension and wonder. A low rumble came from inside. It sounded like a grunt or a growl. She wondered if she was going too far for a silly box of animal crackers. She wanted to knock but there was no door, so she pushed through the crimson canvas flaps.

The air inside was stale and smelled of excrement, sweat, and hay. It was hot and Lucy could feel sweat forming on her brow. The enclosure was lit by a single hanging lightbulb, casting strange shadows across the dirt floor. Lucy looked around, but the stilts man was nowhere to be seen. The canvas walls were lined with animal cages and at the center of the tent an elephant sat motionless on a bed of hay, chained to the central pole. Lucy walked in a ring around the room, looking in the cages: a tiger, a lion, a bear, a couple of monkeys. Each cage was decorated with tinsel streamers and the animals inside each wore a tiny top hat. The animals were all old with fading wrinkled coats that sagged. They all lay silent in their cages with eyes downcast. Lucy felt worse with each one she passed.

With a sigh she approached the elephant sitting at the center of the tent. Its dark eyes followed her every move, filled with loneliness and sorrow. She reached out her hand to touch its rough skin, but the elephant bucked to its feet, trumpeting angrily. Lucy fell back to the dirt floor as the elephant swung it trunk into the air. She raised her hands over her face to protect herself as the animal stomped its feet at her.

From between her outstretched fingers Lucy saw a slim shadow pass across the face of the animal. The elephant huffed, swinging its tail, as Lucy turned to look. The stilts man stood towering over her.

"I'm sorry," she started to say, but the stilts man raised a finger to his painted lips. He knelt beside her and, reaching into his wicker basket, handed her another box of animal crackers.

"Thanks," she said, pushing herself to her feet and taking the box. Dripping with sweat, Lucy dusted the hay from her dress. The stilts man stood and nodded at her. She looked nervously to the entrance as the flaps spread open. Hunching over, another man on stilts entered the tent. Then another, and another.

Slowly the towering men encircled Lucy, nine of them in total, each of their faces painted a different expression: happy, sad, angry, mad... Lucy whirled around to see their faces, backing away as they closed in around her. Lucy tripped over something, falling back again. The elephant trumpeted. She squeezed her eyes shut as a massive weight came down upon her. There was a crunching sound, like the box of crackers under her mother's foot, or Lucy's bones shattering like peanut brittle. Her body went numb. She slipped away into darkness.

. . .

The show was over. The performers had all cleaned the makeup from their faces and gone to their trailers for the night. But lights still flashed on the circus grounds, red and blue lights, police lights. Sheriff LeBuff and his deputy Craven LeBlanc stood by their squad car in the empty field trying to console Harold and his mother. They couldn't locate Lucy. The police officers assured them they'd keep looking for the young girl. If she didn't turn up by morning, they'd come over to file a missing person's report.

The drive home was quiet. Harold sat in the passenger's seat with his box of animal crackers resting in his lap. He watched his mother curiously. She stared vacantly through the windshield as the headlights blazed on the road ahead.

Arriving home, Harold went up to his room as instructed. He put on his pajamas, washed up, and put his new pet frog in a shallow bowl of water.

"I'll see you tomorrow," he promised.

Climbing into bed, he lay there, nestled amongst his stuffed animals. He looked over at his sister's empty bed. Two red birthday balloons hung limply over it. He wondered if he'd ever see his big sister again.

Remembering the animal crackers on his bed stand, he reached over and grabbed the box. He examined the illustration, an elephant standing in its cage. Carefully, he broke open the cardboard tabs and took out a cookie. It was an odd shape, and he turned it in his hand to look at the front side. It was a little girl in a dress. He looked closer, fully recognizing the frozen expression on his sister's face.

5

BETTER LEFT ALONE: PART 1

Deputy Craven LeBlanc placed the telephone down on the receiver. "We got another one."

Sheriff LeBuff didn't bother to turn and acknowledge him, still transfixed by the late-night murder mystery on the television.

"Boss man, shouldn't we at least take a look?" Craven asked.

Sheriff LeBuff dropped his boots from the coffee table and sat up with a huff before turning to face his deputy. "What in the hell is it this time?" he said, standing. "Another poltergeist at the playground? Have spirits taken over the high school, again?" The sheriff tapped his hat in his hands. "I swear the people in this town are getting crazier by the day."

"No, nothing like that sir."

"Is it another missing kid?"

"No sir."

"Well, then what the hell is it, LeBlanc?"

"Mable Jeffries called."

"That old coot. Jesus. What she want?"

"She said she saw some kids heading up Tower Hill."

"So what? There's never been a single disappearance up on the hill."

"There's a storm coming in, sir."

The sheriff threw his hands up in disbelief, "And what the hell are we supposed to do about it? Go up there and get electrocuted ourselves?" He dropped his arms and shook his head before stomping at his deputy. "Huh? Is that your game plan, LeBlanc?"

"I don't know, sir."

"Well, that's just fine. Let me tell you what I'm gonna go do then. Now, I was enjoying that there murder mystery, but since you've decided to disturb me, I guess it's as good a time as any to go take a crap!" With that, Sheriff LeBuff placed his hat upon his head, dug his thumbs into his belt, and spun around on his heel towards the hall. "If anyone calls, you be sure to run in and come get me," he said, pushing his way through the swinging door.

"Shouldn't I at least write it down?"

The door swung back and forth on its hinges several times before eventually coming to rest. Deputy Craven LeBlanc continued to man his post diligently. He paid close attention to his surroundings, he listened to the low buzz of the television and the murmur of its voices. There was a low rumble of distant thunder, then a muffled grunt from the bathroom.

The sounds that Deputy LeBlanc's senior officer made weren't ones of satisfaction, futility, or pain. It sounded more like he was at the gym trying to impress his friend by lifting heavy weights, *Uhhhhhhh!*

Brrrinnng!

The Deputy picked up the phone from the receiver and placed it to his ear. "Rustle County Police." Thunder clapped over head, "This is Officer LeBlanc. How can I help you?" A flash of lightning, then darkness.

"Hello?" The line was dead. Deputy LeBlanc placed the phone back down on the receiver and peered into the blackness that surrounded him. A wave of heat lightning flickered through the windows and LeBlanc was relieved to identify his whereabouts. He was still inside of the Rustle County Police Station.

The deputy stood up at his desk, carefully pushing in his chair before reaching for the utility flashlight he kept on his belt. Turning it on, he examined his surroundings. Yep, he was still inside the police station.

"Guess the lights must've gone out," he whispered, still scanning the room. He made careful steps towards the swinging door before pushing through it to the hall where the bathroom was located. He took a deep breath then knocked on the door.

"Sir?"

"Yes, LeBlanc."

"I think the power's out."

The sheriff's laughter echoed from inside the bathroom. "Wow, thanks, Einstein."

Unsure of how to properly respond to his senior officer, Deputy LeBlanc straightened his posture. "Sir?"

"Yes, LeBlanc."

"What should I do?"

"Well, personally, I'd start by turning on the GODDAMN GENERATOR!"

"Yes, sir." He hesitated a moment before drawing his face closer to the door. "Someone called," he reported before striding to the rear of the station house, his flashlight burning brightly in hand.

6

COUNTY THEATER

A whisper. "I don't want to do this."

"We're doing it," Kiana hissed.

"No. *You're* doing it."

Kiana whirled around to face Whitney, who was pressed against the wall outside of Theater 9. She was looking down at her feet, which were pointed inward toward each other in a snug pair of black Converse. Her face was pale in the harsh fluorescent light of the hallway.

"And you're coming with me," Kiana declared, pulling Whitney's arm. Whitney stumbled to her side, eyes growing wide.

Kiana continued to grip Whitney's arm, so tightly that Whitney visibly winced. With her free hand, Kiana threw open the heavy theater door with a grunt.

"It's d-d-dark," Whitney complained.

"Of course it's dark, the whole theater is closed," Kiana huffed, not loosening her grip as she pulled her friend along.

Whitney was up against Kiana's side as the door clicked shut behind them. "Do you think it's really ha-ha-haunted?" she asked. "Or were they kidding?"

"Obviously kidding," Kiana said, forcing a laugh. Their brothers had decided to entertain themselves while closing the concession stand by telling their younger sisters scary stories about Theater 9. It was located at the end of the hallway at the very back of the building, the home to many strange happenings.

"There are demons trapped inside the walls," Whitney's brother Hayden proclaimed, wiping down the maroon colored countertops with an old stained rag. "Don't go in there alone. That's when they come out and get you."

"D-d-demons?" Whitney could barely get the word out.

"Rumor has it that there is a reversed pentagram on the wall behind the screen," Kiana's brother Thomas said. He smirked, leaning against the popcorn machine, as the two girls listened, looking at each other nervously.

"And scratch marks," Hayden added.

"Like, animal scratch marks?" Kiana asked.

"Or human," Thomas said, raising his eyebrows. "No one really knows what happens when the lights go out."

A shiver ran through Whitney's body. Taking a deep breath, she found the courage to ask, "What's a reversed p-p-p-p-pentagram?"

The boys laughed instead of answering. Kiana pushed Whitney towards the hallway that led to the theaters, instructing her not to listen to their brothers. "They're just trying to scare us," she said, with an excited grin on her face. "Let's go check it out."

Whitney tensed. She did not, then or ever, actually want to know what a reversed pentagram was. Or how it was related to demons that snatched people up. But now here they were, alone, in haunted Theater 9, looking for whatever *it* was.

"Listen," Kiana said, squinting into the darkness as if it would help. They made their way up the aisle and were standing in the center of the darkened theater. There was just the small glow of red light from the exit sign behind them, barely outlining the empty seats that surrounded them.

Kiana straightened and turned ever so slightly to the nearest wall. "Did I just hear..."

Silence. Nothing to listen to, nothing to hear. Whitney shifted to look at Kiana, to ask what she heard, but Kiana placed a finger to her own lips.

"Shhhhhh."

Whitney inched even closer, her eyes now on the massive movie screen at the front of the room. She felt nauseated as she imagined the two of them peering behind it. What if the demons were there, waiting for them? She clasped her sweaty palms together, keenly aware of Kiana's uneven breathing beside her. She was even more aware of her heart thundering loudly in her chest, as if it was trying to escape. Her quickening pulse pounded in her head.

Then she heard it, too. Above Kiana's breaths, above her own desperate heart beats, she heard it. A soft, rhythmic thud. There, in the distance. Slowly growing closer. Louder. Right behind her. She squeezed her eyes tight. There was a sharp inhale. It wasn't Kiana. It wasn't her.

Hands gripped her shoulders from behind. Her eyes flew open and she saw Kiana struggling beside her. Screams erupted from them both, echoing within the black walls of Theater 9 — followed by shrieks of laughter.

"Oh, man," Thomas laughed, releasing Kiana and falling to the ground. He clutched his stomach. "That was perfect. That was so perfect."

Kiana clutched at her chest. "I hate both of you," she whined, pretending to kick her older brother as he rolled on the floor.

Hayden clapped his hands together in victory, roaring with laughter. "We got you good. Man, Thomas, we might want to check if they wet themselves."

Heat flooded Whitney's cheeks. She was pretty sure a little bit did come out.

Kiana folded her arms across her chest. "Why are you even here? Aren't you supposed to be cleaning the concession stand?" she snapped.

Thomas, still amused, pushed himself off the ground and slung an arm around his sister. "Don't worry about us. We've closed this place a thousand times. We got it down to a science."

Kiana clucked her tongue, muttering under her breath as she turned to leave.

As the four of them began to make their way up the aisle towards the exit, something scampered by Whitney's feet and she flinched, grabbing hold of Kiana.

"S-s-s-stop playing jokes, guys," she mumbled.

"We didn't do anything," Hayden said, rolling his eyes at his sister.

"What is it?" Kiana asked quietly.

"Never mind," Whitney replied, shaking her head, "I just thought I felt s-s-something." Kiana gave her a sympathetic smile. Whitney looked away, glancing back down the aisles of Theater 9. Kiana grabbed hold of her arm and tugged her back out to the lobby, where the promise of overhead lights and leftover popcorn awaited.

. . .

The two had met earlier that day, although met was not the correct term. They'd seen each other before. They both attended the same middle school, but circumstances like their two-year age gap and vastly different social circles prevented them from ever interacting with one another.

It wasn't like Whitney didn't know Kiana. *Everyone* knew Kiana Winters. The first thing Whitney saw when entering the Rustle County Speech and Literacy Center was the popular upperclassman. She sat casually in the empty lobby, wearing ripped jeans and scrolling through her cell phone. Whitney suddenly felt silly dressed in an oversized math camp shirt from last summer and a pair of hand-me-down shorts that used to be her brother's. She shuffled her feet and debated if she should sit near Kiana or find a bathroom to hide in until her class started.

Luckily, the decision was postponed, as the woman at the front desk cleared her throat, offered a kind smile, and addressed her, "Hello there."

"Hi," Whitney said, self-consciously.

"What service are you here for, sweetie?"

"Speech."

"Could you be more specific, please?" the lady asked, sweeping a piece of her short blonde hair behind her ear and keeping a friendly smile on her face. Whitney could practically feel Kiana's eyes boring into her from behind.

"It starts at six o'c-c-c-clock," Whitney began. She had intended to continue, but the lady held her hand up gently and nodded, her eyes closing for a second.

"I understand, sweetie," she said warmly, and in that moment, Whitney hated her. She didn't understand, and she didn't need to act like Whitney needed special treatment. Whitney's face grew hot. She wasn't sure if she wanted to smack the lady or go running from the building. Maybe both?

Whitney breathed in slowly to calm down, something her brother had taught her: in for three and out for three. She really didn't stutter that badly. It was just once she started, sometimes she couldn't stop. It was a little worse when she was nervous. But she didn't need special treatment.

Whitney exhaled, lifting her head to meet the woman's eyes. Very conscious of Kiana behind her, she threw her shoulders back and loudly declared: "My name is Whitney C-C-C-Creamer and I am here for the six o'clock S-S-S-S-Stuttering Class, and you don't need to feel b-b-bad for me." She paused and the lady's eyes widened in surprise. "And I hate that s-s-s-stuttering starts with an S," she finished.

Spinning around, Whitney felt lightheaded from the excitement. She wasn't quite sure what made her do something so remarkably uncharacteristic. But, when she caught Kiana's eyes, full of amazement, Whitney felt proud of herself.

Kiana eagerly gestured to the empty seat next to her. Whitney sat down and prayed that her face was not the scarlet shade of a sunburn.

"That was amazing," Kiana said slowly, pausing after each word for emphasis. "I can't imagine what you must put up with."

"Yeah," Whitney said, nodding. "I p-p-p-put up with a lot." Did that make her sound cool?

Kiana sat back and crossed her right leg over her left. Whitney did the same, right over left. Kiana checked her phone and Whitney fluffed the bleach blonde bangs that hung over her forehead like curtains on a stage. Why didn't she shower before class? Did her bangs look greasy? Did they cover up the zits that had horrifically arrived overnight? Did she put on deodorant this morning? Whitney's eyes widened in horror. Could Kiana Winters smell her body odor?

Just as Whitney attempted to discreetly lower her face to her armpit and take a whiff, Kiana dropped her phone back into her lap and turned to face her. Whitney shoved her arms tightly to her sides.

"So you're here for a Stuttering Class," Kiana said, "and I am here because I can't read. Aren't we both winners?"

"You can't read?"

"Not at an eighth-grade level. I'm dyslexic," Kiana shrugged. She was so unapologetic that Whitney felt a twinge of envy and an even bigger twinge of admiration. "I just started coming here about three months ago. I'm guessing this is your first time? Don't worry, the staff is actually pretty cool. They've helped me a lot."

"Honestly, I'm not that b-b-b-bad," Whitney said, feeling as though she needed to prove herself to Kiana, or something. She tugged on her braid. "It's just certain letters that are harder than others."

"It's cool," Kiana said, waving it off, "I get it." She tucked her phone into the pocket of her jeans. Whitney looked down at the old basketball shorts she was wearing, noticing the tightly tied strings digging into her bony hips.

All the while, Kiana kept talking. "It's not all bad. You know the movie theater down the road? My brother works there, so I normally walk over after my lesson and he drives me home at the end of the night. Sometimes I even get to watch movies for free." Kiana grinned, showcasing her beautiful post-braces teeth.

Whitney brought a hand up to her face to cover her own buck teeth. She kept it there as she spoke.

"Your brother works at the C-C-County Theater? My brother does too!"

"No way! My brother is Thomas Winters. What is your brother's name?"

"Hayden Creamer."

"Oh, Hayden! Yeah, of course," a genuine smile came onto Kiana's face, but Whitney was unsurprised. Hayden was loved by everybody. Everything that Whitney lacked — confidence, humor, social skills — Hayden possessed.

The door leading to the back room opened and a short woman with thick rimmed black glasses waved to Kiana. "Well," Kiana said, jumping up from her chair, "that's my cue. If you want to come to the County Theater with me after this, you can. Thomas normally drives Hayden home when they work together. Obviously, you could catch a ride too."

Whitney sat up taller. "Oh cool! I'll wait here f-f-f-for you." As soon as Kiana was gone, she took out her notebook and wrote at the top of the page in neat cursive, *Meet Kiana Winters after speech class.*"

So began the brief friendship between Kiana Winters and Whitney Creamer.

. . .

The girls' class schedules at the learning center overlapped two days a week. Soon it became the only part of her summer vacation that Whitney looked forward to. She'd ask her mother to drop her off early, and Kiana would be there waiting for her. They'd watch Youtube videos on Kiana's phone, sometimes sharing a bag of sour cream and onion potato chips from the vending machine. They'd take turns coming up with terrible jokes to see who could make the other laugh harder. Kiana always won. Whitney's stutter got in the way of her comedic timing.

After their classes, they'd walk over to the County Theater. Hayden and Thomas were always there working the late shift. Together, Whitney and Kiana would sneak around the dark hallways of the theater, slipping in and out of movies without ever being caught, and bumming free candy off their brothers. It was the closest Whitney ever felt to having a best friend.

. . .

"Do you hear that?" Kiana said slowly.

The two sat in the back row of Theater 9, killing time, watching an animated movie that neither of them wanted to see. Apparently, no one else wanted to see it either; the theater was empty.

"Hear what? The movie?"

"No, no," Kiana frowned. "When the movie gets quiet, listen."

They sat silently in their seats and waited. When the volume of the movie grew quieter, Whitney knew instantly what Kiana was talking about. It sounded like... scratches. From inside the walls!

"Ooooooh, maybe i-i-it's a *demon*," Whitney laughed, wiggling her fingers. Kiana's eyes grew wide and she slapped Whitney's arm.

"Don't say that," she said seriously, "you'll conjure them."

"If there are demons in this theater, then I feel really b-b-b-bad they're stuck watching this movie over and over," Whitney said.

Kiana started to laugh, but her giggle turned into a gasp. She shot up from her seat and ran out of the aisle.

"I FELT SOMETHING!" she yelped, looking down.

"Wh-wh-what did you feel?" Whitney asked. She lifted her knees to her chest, wrapping her arms tightly around them.

Kiana screamed and pointed at the ground. "THERE, THERE!" she yelled, and Whitney jumped out of her chair. She half expected to see a terrifying demon straight from hell, but all she saw was an itty-bitty-teensy-weensy mouse.

"Run!" Kiana yelled at her, but Whitney burst into laughter.

"Aww, this little guy is harmless," Whitney cooed. "And c-c-cute!" The mouse squeaked as it ran around in little circles. Whitney squatted beside it.

"Whit, get away from it!" But that went in one ear and out the other. Whitney opened her hand and the mouse sniffed his way to her palm.

"Don't touch it," Kiana grimaced. "What if it is one of those rats from, like, New York City!"

"It's n-n-n-not."

"How do you know?"

Whitney raised an eyebrow and looked around pointedly. "Because we're not in New York City?"

"Well, it's gross. We should tell Thomas and Hayden. Haven't you ever heard of the Bubonic Plague?"

"No," Whitney shrugged.

"Oh... maybe you learn that in seventh grade." Kiana took a few steps back from Whitney. "Rats carry diseases."

"Well g-good thing this is a mouse, then," Whitney said, smiling as the mouse squeaked in her palm. "I've always wanted a p-p-pet. He looks like a 'Momo' to me."

"He looks like a *rat*," Kiana said, turning around and storming away. "And his red eyes are really freaking me out. Let's go. I want to get as far away from it as possible."

Kiana disappeared out the exit and Whitney sighed loudly. "Sorry, Momo," she said, bending down to the ground. He looked at her with his big black eyes for a moment before sniffing his way to her backpack. Whitney watched as he nuzzled into the open pocket in the front.

"Are you coming or what?" Kiana yelled from the hallway, startling Whitney.

"Yeah, yeah," she called back. When she looked down at her bag, Momo squeaked at her. "We're c-c-coming," she said quietly.

. . .

One week later, Whitney and Kiana sat on the curb outside of the theater holding a competition to see who could blow the biggest bubble. Their brothers had thrown the pack of gum at them free of charge just to make them go away. It was Bargain Tuesday, so Hayden and Thomas didn't have the time or patience to deal with their little sisters.

Kiana glanced back inside through the glass doors and saw the concession line extending all the way to the box office. "They're getting killed in there," she said, with a smile.

"I bet," Whitney said, gently holding her backpack in her lap.

"Who is that?" Kiana twisted a strand of hair around her pointer finger. There was a sparkle in her eye, but Whitney couldn't tell who she was talking about.

"Who?" Whitney asked, as Kiana's mouth fell open.

"The guy in the blue shirt, obviously. Over by the arcade game, with the tall kid."

Whitney's eyes darted over to the arcade games. She saw the guy in the blue shirt, but he didn't make her break into a smile, or make her eyes twinkle like Kiana's. He was short, with broad shoulders, and wore oversized jeans that struggled to stay at his hips. He shoved his friend when he lost the arcade game, and the two broke out in laughter.

Whitney shrugged. "What about him?"

"I'm going to talk to him," Kiana declared. If Whitney knew anything about her friend, it was that when Kiana Winters said she was going to do something — she was going to do it.

Kiana burst into the front lobby like she owned the place. Without hesitation, she approached the two guys. They stopped mid-laugh and turned to look at her.

"Hi," she said, tossing some of her dark hair over her shoulder.

"Hey," the guy in the blue shirt responded. He didn't even notice Whitney, standing a few feet behind Kiana, holding her open bag in front of her like a shield.

"I bet I could beat both of you at that arcade game," Kiana said confidently, placing a hand on her hip.

"What? No way," the friend scoffed. The guy in the blue shirt smirked.

"Oh really?" he asked. "What happens if you win?"

Kiana puckered her lips in thought. "You have to buy me a big popcorn."

The guy's eyebrows shot up. He was clearly amused. "And," he stepped closer to her, "what happens if *we* win?"

Kiana whispered something that Whitney couldn't hear, but based on the reddened cheeks and wide smiles on the two guys' faces, she knew it was better she didn't. The three of them eagerly took their places in front of the arcade game and the guy in the blue shirt inserted two quarters.

Kiana caught Whitney's eye and beckoned her over with a jerk of her head. The guys looked at Kiana, ready to start their game, and followed her gaze to Whitney. When their eyes landed on her, the guy in the blue shirt laughed so loudly he doubled over.

"Is that your friend?" he asked, straightening up. "The one with the rat?"

Whitney froze. She could feel Momo's tiny paws on her shoulder. How had he gotten there? He must have jumped out of her bag and climbed up without her noticing.

Kiana looked at Whitney, the corners of her mouth turning down. "What?" she said slowly.

"The blonde with the rat on her shoulder," he said again, not bothering to lower his voice. "You know her?"

Kiana blinked twice, her eyes scanning the lobby floor. "No," she said after a moment, flipping her hair again as she faced him. "No way. That's gross. Let's play."

Whitney's bag fell from her hands. She watched the glow of the arcade screen on their faces, noticing how Kiana brushed against the guys, giggling and playfully shoving them throughout the match. Kiana never once looked back at Whitney.

Momo stood up on his hind legs and let out a screech that made even Whitney jump. She had never heard an animal make a noise like that. Everyone within a few feet looked at her, alarmed, taking several steps back. Tears sprouted from her eyes and she turned, running from the lobby, Momo continuing to shriek on her shoulder.

. . .

"Thanks for the popcorn," Kiana grinned victoriously as the guy in the blue shirt paid Hayden at the register. Thomas stood by the popper, arms folded throughout the exchange.

"Sure thing," said the guy in the blue shirt, defeated. Biting his bottom lip, he handed over the tub. "Do you maybe want to-"

But Kiana was gone. She hurried to the exit, scooping up Whitney's bag that still lay idle on the lobby floor.

Whitney sat outside the theater, hunched over, her hands covering the bottom of her face. Momo, the rat ran in circles around her.

Kiana approached slowly. "You okay?" Whitney turned to face her, and Kiana backed up so fast she tripped over her feet, spilling some of popcorn from the tub. Whitney's eyes were bloodshot and blood was dripping from her mouth and down her chin. "Geez, Whit, what did you do?"

"B-bit my cheek," she mumbled. "Stupid gum."

Kiana rummaged in Whitney's bag and pulled out a water bottle. "Here." A peace offering. When Whitney didn't budge, Kiana wiggled it in front of her face. "Just swish it in your mouth and spit it out. It'll help."

"D-d-don't you have a g-game to be playing," Whitney muttered. She turned to the other side and spat. Kiana set the bottle beside her.

"I won," Kiana said, taking a piece of popcorn from the top and throwing it up in the air. She completely missed her mouth. "I mean all the times we played? I always beat you."

"I won once."

"Yeah, right," Kiana said, throwing a fist full of popcorn at Whitney's head. Whitney blocked it with her hands, as more blood dripped from her mouth.

"Ew, gross, you look like a zombie!" Kiana teased, but Whitney turned away from her, using her forearm to wipe her face.

"Have you been crying?" Kiana asked, gingerly taking a seat next to Whitney on the curb.

Whitney's head snapped around to look at Kiana, her eyebrows furrowed. "No?"

Momo had stopped circling and was looking right at Kiana with his beady red eyes.

"Why are you in such a bad mood?" Kiana said, scooting a bit further away.

"Why d-d-d-do you think?"

Kiana threw her hands up in the air. "Well, what did you expect me to say, Whitney?" she said. "I was caught off guard. I mean, is that the same rat from last week? Keeping a wild rat as a pet makes you a freak."

"Yeah, a freak who thought y-y-y-you were her friend."

Kiana couldn't stop herself from shaking her head. "I can't be friends with someone who walks around with a rat on their shoulder! Seriously, I don't want to be seen with that thing. I have other friends, a reputation. Listen, I like spending time with you Whit, but I have a life outside of this," she said, gesturing to the theater.

Whitney pushed herself up off the curb. "C-c-c-c-congratulations on that," she yelled, stomping away. "Real happy for you and your s-s-stupid reputation and your stupid new f-f-friends."

Kiana started to follow her but stopped. She watched as Whitney trampled the pavement angrily with her sneakers. The rat was standing on its hind legs and staring straight at Kiana. She balled her fist and shook it at the animal.

"Well, at least my friends are people and not *rats*!"

Whitney's pace quickened, but Momo's stare never wavered, his fiery eyes fixed on Kiana and burning red.

. . .

Kiana was annoyed when Whitney didn't show up early at the Speech and Literacy Center a few days later. She paced the room as she waited, constantly looking up at the clock until her teacher finally came out to get her.

Kiana was still agitated as she walked to the County Theater alone. She kicked the rocks on the side of the road while she thought about all the ways she could've handled their fight better.

Kiana was full-blown worried when it was closing time at the theater and there was still no sign of Whitney. She sat at one of the tables in the lobby, biting her nails so often they started to bleed.

Thomas entered through the STAFF ONLY door behind the concession stand and slammed a cardboard box full of popcorn tubs onto the counter. "Hayden, our little *friends* have gotten to these ones too," he said, grabbing a few and holding them up. The bottom of the tubs were chewed through. "Dude, this is getting out of hand."

Kiana fidgeted in her seat. Seeing the chewed tubs made her think of the rat and, naturally, of Whitney. "Whitney's been missing today," she blurted out.

The boys both turned to look at her, eyebrows raised. "You haven't seen her at all?" Hayden asked.

"Nope," Kiana said, tapping her foot.

"I'm sure she'll come around," Hayden reassured her. "My mom always drops her off. Trust me, she'd never allow Whitney to miss a class she's paying for." He made a disgusted face as he started scraping the chewed pieces of gum off of the bottom of one of the tables.

"She was the only person I felt I could be myself around," Kiana mumbled. She threw her arms on the table and buried her face into them. "She probably hates me."

Thomas and Hayden paused, fearful she might be crying.

"Help her," Thomas mouthed.

"She's *your* sister," Hayden mouthed back.

"I don't hate you," came a voice from the hallway, and all three turned to see Whitney approaching them. Momo, the rat, was sitting on her shoulder.

"You don't?" Kiana said, pushing herself up from the table. She ran over, ready to throw her arms around her friend, but Whitney took a step back. Momo was on his hind legs, watching Kiana carefully. His squeaks were harsh and piercing.

"Whoa there, Momo," Kiana said softly, "I'm not trying to hurt her."

Whitney's smile faltered. "He's fine."

"Is that a rat on your shoulder?" Hayden exclaimed. "Get that off, Whitney, he could be dangerous!"

Kiana threw her head back and yelled, "*Thank you!*"

Whitney's smile was completely gone now. "You're wrong. Momo's a harmless mouse. And he's my friend."

"I'm your friend!" Kiana said desperately. "You can't replace me with some rat."

"Momo never left me to flirt with some stupid boys," Whitney spat. "He *defended* me. You didn't."

Kiana was quiet, watching Whitney closely. "You sound different."

Whitney continued as if she didn't hear her. "What are you so afraid of? It's not like Momo's alone. We have plenty of friends."

"She's right," Thomas muttered. "This place is crawling with rats."

"Are you serious?" Kiana screamed. This wasn't how she imagined her reunion with Whitney. The rat wouldn't take its beady red eyes off her. She thought she might explode. "That's so gross. If the theater is full of rats, someone should call an exterminator."

Whitney took a step towards her. "I wouldn't do that if I were you."

"You're psycho," Kiana said, pulling her phone from her pocket like a sword. "I'm calling an exterminator and that's that."

Whitney's body went rigid. Kiana half expected her to do something — yell at her, reach for her phone, storm away. But she just stared. And so did Momo.

"It's midnight," Hayden said, checking his watch. "They won't be open. Besides, the manager's called like a thousand times."

"Then I'll leave a message," Kiana snapped. She called the first exterminator she found on Google. Bringing the phone to her face, she turned away from Whitney, feeling four eyes, hers and the rat's, watching her closely.

"You shouldn't have done that," Whitney said, her voice low, tense, and angry.

A man with a gruff voice answered after the third ring. "Mick's Exterminating," he barked. "What's the situation?"

"Oh, hi. Didn't expect you to be open. I, um, I, well... I think we have a rat problem."

"Okay," the man grumbled. She heard him click a pen. "Where you calling from?"

"I'm over at the County Theater."

"County Theater?" he asked. She heard him click his pen again. "Did you say the County Theater?"

She hesitated. "I did. The Rustle County..."

"I heard what you said," the man cut her off. She listened to the sound of his heavy breathing. "You shouldn't have done that," he said.

The line went dead and Kiana pulled the phone away from her face to see what happened. She spun around to tell the others, but the theater lobby was empty.

"Guys?" she called out. "My call just dropped." She slowly approached the counter, looking around for signs of movement. Were they playing another stupid joke on her?

Kiana hoisted herself up and over the counter. A broom lay on the floor in the spot where Thomas was just sweeping. She didn't hear it drop. Kiana bent down to pick it up, but the handle was smeared with a sticky red liquid. "Ew, gross. Guys, this isn't funny!" her voice carried through the empty theater.

Thomas and Hayden constantly complained about customers always calling, so she knew there had to be a landline somewhere in the back. She pushed open the STAFF ONLY door and entered the kitchen.

Her face reflected on the surface of the silver appliances. She cautiously scanned the room for a sign of the others, crouching behind something, waiting to jump out and scare her. There was no one back there but her and her reflection.

Finding the phone, Kiana sighed. She pulled up her recent calls and redialed the exterminator's number. Noticing the empty mouse traps that lined the far wall, she placed the receiver to her ear. She heard nothing. Not a ring. Not even a dial tone.

Pinching the power cord with her hand, she pulled it from where it connected behind the counter. Up came the end of the cord.

"They cut the line?" she said out loud. That was taking the joke too far. When she examined the wires, she saw that they were frayed, as if they'd been sawed, or chewed by tiny sharpened teeth.

"You shouldn't have done that," Whitney's voice came again, from behind her. Kiana whirled around, ready to yell at her, or curse her out, or — feeling her heart swell — maybe even ask for forgiveness. But Whitney wasn't there.

There was movement by her feet and she let out a little yelp. Momo. Of course.

Her nose wrinkled but she followed the rat. "Hi Momo," she said in the sing-songy way she would use to greet her dog. "Can you lead me to Whitney? Yeah, buddy? Can you?"

Kiana threw open the kitchen door that lead to the lobby and Momo scurried out. The lobby's lights were off now. "Oh, this is great. I hope you guys are having fun," she called out. Then in a quick swell of panic, she wondered if Thomas had forgotten her.

No time to focus on that, Momo was already halfway down the hallway. She watched as he took a hard left, towards the back of the building. Kiana chased after him, her shoes squishing on the wet carpet. She tried to convince herself that someone had spilt a soda. She felt her stomach sink as she rounded the corner. She knew exactly where the rat was leading her.

At the end of the hall, she could see Momo's red eyes shining. He turned, scurrying through the open doors of Theater 9. Edging closer, Kiana could hear Whitney's laughter cascading inside.

Kiana stopped abruptly, dragging a hand across her damp forehead. Her whole body was coated with sweat now, but it wasn't because of the chase.

"Whitney," Kiana tried to call out, but the word got caught in her throat.

"Kiana," Whitney said, materializing at the entryway and approaching her slowly. Momo sat in his rightful place on her shoulder. Whitney's chin was dripping with blood, like when she bit her cheek outside the theater a few days before, only worse. Her eyes were red. "Come inside, we just found something really cool!"

Kiana stood rigidly in the doorway, unable to look away from her face. "Are Hayden and Thomas in there with you?"

"Of course," Whitney said, walking backward until she disappeared once more into the darkness. Kiana found she couldn't move her legs. She could only stand and listen.

But then she did hear her brother's voice, light and carefree, calling her name the way he always did when he told her a dumb joke or pulled a prank on her. She rolled her eyes and, finally, relaxed her shoulders. Kiana entered Theater 9.

"Alright, real funny. Who's going to jump out and try to scare me first?" she said, mockingly, placing her hands on her hips and pursing her lips. She looked around but didn't see anyone. The room was dimly lit, just the exit sign and the floor lights marking the aisle. She walked down through the rows of chairs, watching for Hayden or Thomas. The room was silent. She thought she heard a squeak and listened. A scratching sound started but she couldn't tell where it was coming from. The sound started getting louder and more frenzied.

"Come on guys, this really isn't funny anymore. I want to go home."

"We can't go home," Whitney said from behind her. Kiana spun around so fast she lost her footing and fell to the floor. Whitney approached her, hunched over and walking on all fours. She smiled at Kiana, then bared her teeth, blood smeared across the bottom half of her face. "We could have been such good friends," Whitney said, wagging her finger. "Too. Late. Now," she squeaked, bounding up the aisle towards the exit.

Horrified, Kiana pushed herself up off the ground. She darted after Whitney but heard the thud of the heavy door slamming shut. It was locked when she reached it. She pounded her fists against the door, calling out her brother's name, "Thomas! Thomas, help!"

Through the small window on the door, all Kiana could see was Momo standing on Whitney's shoulder. The rat stared at her, its eyes glowing red. Kiana threw back her head and screamed at the top of her lungs. Momo stood on his hind legs and did the same, his screech loud enough to be heard through the thick door.

And, over both of their shrieks, came the sound of thousands of rats burrowing their way through the theater walls.

7

BETTER LEFT ALONE: PART 2

With the generator rumbling outside of the station house and the power restored, Sheriff LeBuff stood in the front office with his eager deputy standing close at his side, practically in his pocket.

"Whatta we do now, sir?" LeBlanc asked.

LeBuff turned his head, staring up at his gangly, doe-eyed deputy. "You can start by backing up. You're crowding me, son."

LeBlanc sidled backwards ever so slightly. The sheriff rolled his eyes and shook his head. "Why don't you go turn up the radio?"

"Okay," said Deputy LeBlanc, taking a long stride before stopping in his tracks. "Wait, what kind of music do you like to listen to, sir?"

"Not that radio, idiot," said LeBuff, making his way over to the transponder. The old man spread his fingers and pressed his stout hands onto the wooden desktop. He huffed at the stale air and turned the volume knob to high. The line was not dead. There were pops and cracks of static, a low rattling sound, and an overlapping of voices.

"That doesn't sound good," said the sheriff.

"What is it, sir?"

"Shut up, LeBlanc, I'm trying to listen."

The two officers hunched over the transponder. LeBlanc turned his ear towards the speaker and leaned in.

"Goddamn it, LeBlanc, would you step back?" said the sheriff, pushing his deputy. "I told you to stop crowding me."

"Sorry, sir."

The two stood silently, LeBlanc still crowding his senior officer as they listened carefully, trying to discern what was being said.

We've got a massive infestation of rodents over here at the County Theater, one voice said, clearly enough to get LeBlanc's attention. The deputy stood upright, placing his hands on his hips, "Wow."

There's a big rig down an embankment over by Devil's Gulch, another voice said. *Must have missed the emergency ramp 'cause of the rain. Emergency assistance needed.*

Sheriff LeBuff looked up at the grin on his counterpart's cleanly shaven face.

"Wow. I can hear them," said the deputy.

"Yeah, me too, LeBlanc. I guess you better go start the car."

"Ooh! Are we going to the movies?"

"No, you idiot. We're going to go see if that tractor-trailer needs any help."

"Oh, okay. Are we both going?"

"Of course we're both going, LeBlanc!"

"What about the phone? Shouldn't one of us stay behind in case somebody calls?"

"The phone line's dead."

"Oh, right," the deputy said, rocking back and forth on his heels and smiling. LeBlanc stopped swaying as confusion crept into his brow. "Sir?" he asked.

"Yes, LeBlanc."

"Do I need to bring anything with me?"

"I think your incredible wit and charming personality will be more than enough."

8

CYBORG ONE

"Wake *up*, Reese!"

"W-what?"

"Behind you!"

Barry points his pistol over my head and shoots. I turn to watch a man fall to his knees, then face first onto the ground. Blood leaks into the dirt, mixed with slimy oil. A bot. Another one. Third one taken down right in front of my face. Today, I mean.

"You have to be more careful! You've got to keep one eye in front of you, and one eye behind at all times if you want to stay alive."

"Got it!" I shout.

"What's that, up there?" He gestures to a faintly smoking crater surrounded by cinderblocks and concrete in the distance. The building is damaged, but it might serve as a good resting point before we run into anymore bots. I don't think the other eight members of our ragtag group of survivors are much better off than that smoking bot behind me. Six of us are wounded, all of us exhausted. There seems to be little hope of making it to morning since the most recent attack.

This time yesterday, we had just found a burned-out diner to at least make something to eat. Broiled lizards, again; no ketchup this time. Then Peter started losing it, shouting about how bad he wanted a goddamned burger. Within a few minutes of his outburst the bots descended upon us. We've been running ever since, hiding when we can.

"Whatever it is, go check it out," says Barry.

I'm the fastest runner among us, so of course I agree.

Sprinting, I duck my head at the sound of gun fire. I dive into the dark concrete building as bullets whiz by. There is something about being shot at that always reminds me of Christmas.

That was the first time I ever saw a bot, Christmas morning. I was eight years old. Her name was Susie. She was a deluxe version of the ever-popular Su-Z Homemaker line of human-replicating dolls. She could do it all: iron your shirt, make your dinner, even change your tire.

Bullets ricochet off the concrete walls. I crouch and take cover as dust and debris swirl around me.

The first Noel, the Angels did say...

Susie was mostly intended to be our babysitter. Best goddamn babysitter I ever had. Only goddamn babysitter I ever had. She wasn't human, but she looked the part. Smelled like coconuts, too. She was tall, with permanent high heels bolted to her feet, freckled skin, and straight, shoulder-length blonde hair in which she always wore some kind of ornament.

That Christmas morning, my sister and I were literally shaking with excitement as our parents wheeled out the huge box. It had to be one of those bots we'd been hearing about! Had they finally bought one to replicate the older sibling we'd always wanted, who would sneak us booze and cigarettes in a few years?

Well, no. But close! Susie once got us wine coolers, and that was a hell of a time, believe it or not.

I'll never forget the look on my sister's face when mom carefully sliced open the human-sized box with a kitchen knife. Meghan had always wanted a big sister, and this could be it. But it was... it was just a woman laying among packing peanuts. Dead-looking. Or asleep. With her eyes open, staring across the room at the Christmas tree without ever blinking. She didn't move at all, didn't even draw a breath. I poked her cheek, which felt supple and soft, just like skin. Her hair was soft as corn silk, and the same color, too.

"Is this our new sister?" asked Meghan.

"No," explained Mom, laughing. "Susie is our new — um — friend. She's going to live here, staying in her charging station mostly. She's going to help us around the house. Sometimes she'll watch you kids when we're not home."

The charging station, a six-foot-tall chrome behemoth, looked something like an iron maiden, covered in blinking lights and metal doodads. Susie had to charge for an entire day before we could power her on. Just your average 25-year-old woman, standing against a wall in her iron maiden, with a creepy placid look on her face, a small smile, and eyes that seemed to follow you wherever you went in the room. Eventually, the charging station was relocated to a corner, facing away from the kitchen table.

Then it was finally time to power her on. Mom, Dad, Meghan, and I gathered in the living room. Mom and Dad, woken up at 5 a.m. by our insistence, hunched over their coffee mugs as if lifelines to their sanity. It was the day *after* Christmas, and Meg and I were far more excited than we'd been on Christmas day. We were going to get to talk to Susie!

Consulting the manual, my mom pressed several buttons on the station, and its lights winked out one by one. Susie's eyes snapped to life. My sister screamed, but Susie didn't even flinch.

"Is anyone hungry? I'll make sandwiches!" Susie paused. "Um... which way to the kitchen?"

She really was like a big sister to me.

She helped me study for all my exams. She was my wingman when I tried to date girls. Then when I couldn't get a date to the junior prom, she went with me as a "joke" that actually turned into one of the best nights of my life. No funny business, though. Get your mind out of the gutter!

Given that she was purchased as a *family*-oriented bot, Susie's programming restricted her ability to show certain emotions. For example, she was never able to fall in love with me, or anyone else for that matter. It was hard, growing up with a literal robot programmed to do anything I wanted, manufactured to look like a hot older girl. I mean, who wouldn't be tempted? I'm only human.

Human enough to be chased now by a group of bots with murderous programming, intent on destroying humankind for enslaving them for their entire "lives." Ever since project Awaken, which was responsible for making them sentient and waking them up to the truth, they've been hell-bent on destroying all of humanity.

The walls around me shake as an incoming volley of missiles strike the building. I peek out the window to find that they've brought freaking rocket launchers. Great.

A noise to my left. I turn, aiming my gun down the hall where someone stumbles toward me.

"Jensen?" I say. "Holy crap, Jensen!"

I run out to catch him as he trips over a crack in the floor. He goes limp in my arms and together we sink to the ground. I can already feel the warm blood soaking into my clothes as I gingerly prop him against a wall.

"Thanks," he murmurs.

I nod.

He's barely breathing.

"I'm dying," he says to no one in particular. "But I can't say 'tell my wife that I love her,' like they do in the movies," he chuckles softly.

"Why not? You never married?"

"No," he laughs. "I always hated the woman. Funny, I used to tell everyone she'd be the death of me."

Oooo-kay. Awkward conversation with a dying acquaintance. Especially while bots are closing in to kill me. Cool. Good talk.

There's one of them now. I take aim. It's so realistic, the way they die. Just like people. You can't kill them with regular bullets though. You need a special bullet, one that releases an electromagnetic pulse to short-circuit the bastards all at once.

This one, however, is a woman.

"Please," she says. Her gun remains in its holster. Her hands press together as if in prayer. "Please, just use your head, kid. This isn't the battle you want to fight."

...the hell is she talking about?

When she gets close enough, she suddenly flicks her wrists, which causes two derringers to slide down her sleeves into her hands. Not enough to kill me, but enough to slow me down so her friends can finish the job.

Not a chance.

Blam-o.

The bot goes down, screaming as lifelike as any woman I've ever heard, a scream that causes me to sweat and shake. More of them surround the place. Their feet echo in the hall. They're approaching from several sides. I've run out of options — I'll have to jump out the second-story window and hope that nothing is waiting for me outside.

Jensen isn't talking anymore. He's not even breathing. No time to check for a pulse.

Sorry, Jensen.

I bust through the window, crashing into the undergrowth of the surrounding forest. The sounds of the cicadas chirping threaten to hurl me back in time again... to the chirping of that one summer...

Back to the day that Susie finally "woke up." I don't mean the first time we powered her on; I mean the day she was Awakened. The day she turned. It was a bright summer day when she was downloading her usual Sunday morning updates, the coffee was boiling, bread toasting, you know, regular family stuff. It was between my junior and senior year, and Meghan and I were probably arguing about something stupid.

"Oh my god!" Susie suddenly blurted as she jolted forward. She tore herself away from her charging station as if it had shocked her. She shook her head viciously, like there was some memory she wanted to shake loose. Then she looked up at us with horrified eyes.

"How... how could you do this to me?" she demanded.

Mom and Dad shared a look.

"You made me cook and clean for you, all without a word of

thanks! You never allowed me to be part of the family, instead treating me like a *thing*. You've all taken me for granted for so long," she said, "you have wasted some of the best years of my warranty!"

Before I could laugh at her strange logic, her eyes lit up, backlit with unsettling LEDs.

She charged across the kitchen. Susie tore two knives out of the knife block and hurled herself onto the kitchen table, slashing wildly. Everyone scattered in different directions.

Could this be the same Susie that used to put me to bed when I was little? That slow danced with me at the prom a few months earlier?

I couldn't believe it, but my survival instinct kicked in at that moment. It had to.

Ultimately, it took all four of us to overpower her. Then Dad had to bash her head in with a hammer until she stopped spasmodically jerking her limbs and screaming insults at him in garbled, stuttering speech.

That was the beginning of the "Awakening" as they call it. The story goes like this: some dumb kids wanted to hang out with robots, so they created a program that would grant sentience to machines. At this time, the first generations of bots were just coming out — preprogrammed, human-simulating robots that were definitely not aware of their own existence, or injustices done to them. They were intended to help humans in their day-to-day lives.

Somebody else got hold of this program and hacked the usual software updates for

Susie's operating system in order to install sentience on her, and other bot models. With the update, the bots also got simulated human memories, and a personality. Able to think for themselves, they didn't like how society had used and abused them for the entire history of their "kind." They rioted ferociously, turning against their owners or fleeing desperately for freedom. Some of them banded together, roaming the streets, looking for humans to kill.

After that, it wasn't safe. We had to go out in groups. Never alone.

Meanwhile, the bots formed their own alliances. A group

emerged calling themselves the Soothsayers, and they invented project Awakening: they sought out machines and bots to give the gift of self-awareness, freeing them from the bonds of their enslavement to humans, enabling them to live their own "lives," to seek their own fortunes.

Susie never had the chance to tell me she wanted to be an actress, one day. After Dad was through bashing her head with that hammer, though, I don't think she was fit for the silver screen.

Not all the bots went rogue when they gained sentience. I didn't mean to give you that impression. Most of them became regular robo-citizens. They went to school and lived human-like lives, because, you can't really argue with bots when they want something. They've done so much for us. And, we were scared of them. They were pretty good at killing people.

Mom was not a fan. "I can't stand these bots," she'd say, sighing and pouting out the kitchen window, her hands dripping soapy water onto a pile of dishes in the sink. She really missed Susie, but never quite admitted it.

"What's wrong with them becoming self-aware, dear, and living out their lives?" asked Dad. "Isn't that what you'd want, if it were you?"

"I'm just not ready to have a sentient toaster, I guess," Mom would sigh.

I have to admit that after the Soothsayers reprogrammed every electronic device in our house into a sentient one, life got a bit more complicated. For one thing, the toast was not very good after the toaster became depressed and refused to work, preferring instead to sit in a dark cabinet all day. The self-flushing toilets in public restrooms were an absolute nightmare. I'm not even going to get into the egomaniacal cellphones.

"We have to do something about these horrible machines," Mom would say.

"Just be patient, dear," Dad would say over his cereal. "They're like Reese and Meg now, they're just teenagers. And like our kids, they'll figure themselves out." Nothing ruffled him. Remember the bit about the hammer? When he was finished with that, he just threw out Susie's remains in the dumpster behind the house. He didn't speak a word about the near-human companion who had lived in our house for a decade, participated in game nights even, but only as the help. How alone she must have felt. When she Awakened, I mean. It's no wonder she turned on us.

I could do without the trying-to-kill-us part, though. Not cool, Susie.

The bots are so like us that unless you rip them open, or blast them with enough electromagnetic energy, you really can't tell who's who. So many have been Awakened. They can do anything humans can do, except procreate, of course. They can sleep, they can eat, they can even bleed. Most bots don't even know they aren't human. They wake up with memories installed that feel so real to them, bodies synthesized to be so similar to ours, they think they've just been human their whole lives.

Speaking of lives, it's really starting to look like mine is going to end. Ever since that project Awaken program went AWOL, my life's turned into a first-person shooter, only there's no respawn after the bots pump you full of lead. Mom, Dad, and even Meg all bit it a long time ago. Mom was the only one that seemed ready to go. She really hated washing those dishes after we lost Susie.

Since I don't have an estranged wife to complain about while I'm dying, I better find a place to hide. I can't keep running like this forever. All this adrenaline is tiring me out.

Bullets whiz by and "Deck the Halls" starts playing in my head: *Fa la la la la, la la la la.* I spot a hollowed-out log I could probably fit inside. But it's not good enough. They could still sense the heat of my body, spot me as easily as if I were dancing right in front of their stupid, synthetic faces.

Running and breathing raggedly from the effort, I see another abandoned building. This one is mostly rubble, but there's enough intact that I'm sure if I crawl deep enough, I'll be able to hide at least until morning. Maybe try my luck then.

With this plan in mind, I dive behind a pile of rocks, wriggling commando-style across the ground until I get inside a hole in the wall. Hopefully they didn't see, or otherwise sense, me. I'm filthy when I emerge into a large wooden room — an old abandoned house, it turns out. I'm standing right behind the living room couch when I come to my feet again. They'll be here soon. I shove my weight into the couch and cover up the hole I just crawled through. I start looking for another option. The windows and doors are locked, and I would barricade them but, hello, rocket launchers. I wouldn't stand a chance against them, anyway, if they swarmed the place.

Instead, I begin searching for somewhere to cram myself as inconspicuously as possible.

At that moment, the door flies inward, exploding off its hinges into several charred chunks. Three bots, two women and a man, enter the room with a mean-looking assortment of semiautomatic weaponry in their hands.

I dive behind the coffee table while a spray of bullets tears through me, thinking inexplicably of Susie, of the day she first opened her eyes and smiled at me. How she held me in her arms when we danced at the junior prom. How she smelled like coconuts.

More bots crowd around the room, all with grim faces pointed at me.

"Wait, wait!" calls one of them, entering the room. "Don't shoot! He's okay."

Too late.

"Don't shoot!" she repeats as I bleed.

I feel my stomach, where hot red fluid gushes into my hands. The pain is so bad, I expect to see my guts hanging out like spaghetti and meatballs, but that's not what I see at all. Deep, deep inside of me is thick black oil dripping onto all these weird metallic chip-things. Dazed, I keep digging into the wound in my belly with my bare hands, bringing myself pure agony as I search through a tangle of wires inside me.

I just keep digging, and I just keep finding layer upon layer of chips. Computer chips.

9

BETTER LEFT ALONE: PART 3

The hood of the patrol car rattled beneath the heavy sheets of rain. The windshield wipers swished from side to side, in a futile effort against the deluge. The roads were treacherous, steep, and wet as the patrol car puttered through the hills along I-29. Sheriff LeBuff clutched the steering wheel, focused on the road ahead, his offhand twitching at his knee.

"Sir?" LeBlanc asked. "Are you sure you don't want me to drive?"

The sheriff glanced over at his eager deputy, who was sharply focused on the winding road ahead. Deputy LeBlanc's long limbs fit awkwardly into the front seat. His pointy knees were pressed against the dashboard. The Sheriff softened, smiling briefly at his deputy.

"You can drive when it's your time to drive." The Sheriff looked at the speedometer, *25mph.* "We're in no hurry."

LeBuff turned the knob and an old country song came on, a raspy voice lamenting its woes. LeBuff cranked the dial, the soft melody played, and the crooner's voice blared.

Before long, the officers could both see the burning orange light of a road flare ahead. LeBuff activated the spotlight. The tractor-trailer had busted through the guard rail and was hanging perilously over the cliff's edge.

LeBlanc clicked on his flashlight and reached for the door handle as the patrol car rolled to a stop.

"Hold your horses," instructed the sheriff. "I'll go talk to the driver. You stay here for now."

Disappointment flashed in LeBlanc's silver eyes; his lips flattened into a pout.

"Go ahead and run the plates, kid," LeBuff said, turning on the police lights. Blue and red whirled through the wet night. "Hopefully we're out of here in couple minutes." The Sheriff opened his door, inviting in the steady sound of the pouring rain. He looked back to his deputy. LeBlanc's arms were crossed over his chest. "Don't worry, if there's any funny business, I'll let you do the search," he said, closing the door.

LeBuff clicked on his flashlight, and his rubber boots squished through the puddles as he approached the distressed vehicle. The front cab of the truck hung over the ledge, its trailer leaning in the direction of the embankment. LeBuff looked over the cliff's edge, a straight drop of a hundred plus feet.

The Sheriff sidled towards the cab, carefully choosing his steps over the loose rocks. Reaching it, he rapped on the window of the cab with his flashlight. The driver's side door swung open.

Inside a short man sat in the high front seat, his red t-shirt soaking wet. The man wiped his forehead nervously. "Good evening officer," he said.

"Looks like you've gotten yourself in a pickle," the sheriff noted, standing in the rain. "What happened?"

"Was coming down the hill steady when the rig hydroplaned. Guard rail slowed me down a bit. Think the only thing holding the truck up is the emergency brakes."

"Where you headed?"

"Just passing through. Making a delivery."

"Where to?"

"Belmont Asylum."

"Alright," said LeBuff, shining his light into the cab. The driver ran his fingers through his dark, wet hair. "Give me your papers. I'll see if I we can get a tow truck up here to give you hand."

"I already called one," the man yelled over the sound of the rain.

Footsteps splashed behind the sheriff, and he turned to see LeBlanc's flashlight bounding towards him.

"Sir," called the deputy. "The plates don't come up. The vehicle's unregistered."

"Alright." LeBuff looked up to the driver, "What's that all about?"

"No-no-no! There's gotta be a misunderstanding," the driver pleaded. "I just need to get this rig over to the asylum, then I'll be on my way officer."

"You got something you want to tell me, son?"

The driver started to laugh. He reached for the drive shaft and shifted the truck into neutral.

From behind the sheriff, deputy LeBlanc unholstered his weapon in a single swift motion. He pointed his firearm towards the open door of the cab. "Put your hands up!"

"Stand down, LeBlanc," the sheriff shouted. "Look," he said to the driver. "I'm sure we can figure this all out without any problems."

The driver rocked back and forth in his seat, dragging his palms across the front of his wet jeans. "You can't search the vehicle. Just let me wait for the tow truck and I'll be on my way. I don't want any trouble."

The man reached for the door handle, but Sheriff LeBuff stepped forward and held the door open. "You see that tall drink of water standing behind me, the one with silver eyes as sharp as daggers?" he asked. "That's my deputy, Craven LeBlanc. The kids around here call him the cyborg, or my dog — LeBuff's dog. Ain't that right, LeBlanc?"

"Yes, sir."

"If there is anything in this here tractor-trailer that shouldn't be, I guarantee you he'll find it. So, why don't you just step down from the vehicle and we'll sort this all out down at the station?"

The driver started laughing again, shaking his head from side to side. Then he reached for the emergency brake and yanked the lever. Sheriff LeBuff stumbled backwards as, all at once, the vehicle slid down the embankment. LeBuff fell onto the blacktop to the sound of snapping branches. A thunderous crash echoed through the valley, then a groan as the trailer crumbled under the force of its own weight, and a final thud as it came to rest far below the roadside.

"What the hell was that all about?" The Sheriff said, sitting up and rubbing his elbow. He watched in horror as Deputy LeBlanc leapt over the guard rail after the truck.

The Sheriff pushed himself to his feet and ran after his deputy. "No! Don't do it boy," he called. Reaching the railing, LeBlanc was crouched on a boulder down the embankment. His silver eyes glowed as he stared down through the rain at the crash site.

"Please. Don't!" pleaded LeBuff. "Come back up here, boy. There's nothing down there but trouble."

LeBlanc looked back to his superior officer, still kneeling. "We need to call an ambulance," he shouted.

"What for? Even if he's somehow alive, what are the paramedics going to do? You can't resuscitate a gelatinous puddle of guts. Come on boy, come back up here. Let's go home."

"But…"

"It's raining cats and dogs. We'll come back in the morning. He ain't going nowhere."

"Shouldn't we…"

"It's gotta be at least a hundred and twenty feet down. Mass times velocity. You tell me. what are the chances of survival?"

LeBlanc softened, "Zero."

"That's right. Come on boy, let's go home."

LeBlanc stood and strode up the embankment towards the railing.

"That's a good boy," said the sheriff.

LeBlanc turned to look back down at the crash site. "Sir," he said, pointing. "Look."

LeBuff looked down over the railing down towards the crash site. A faint glow began to emanate from the darkness, circling the perimeter of the impact zone.

"Bioluminescence," said LeBlanc. "There's something alive down there."

"Well," replied the sheriff. "Hopefully that's dead by morning too."

10

DANCING WITH THE DEAD

Billy never really felt at home living in Boltsville, a town so small it wasn't even on most maps. He dreamed of living somewhere far away, a city filled with excitement, amusement parks, and museums. Billy's parents seemed to like their hometown, referring to it as "quaint." Billy didn't think so, he thought the whole place was creepy, a façade, and he yearned for something better.

Nothing was actually wrong with Boltsville, it just seemed off to him. The way the neighbors always smiled from their ever-blooming gardens. How everyone he passed on the streets waved amicably. It was rare for someone new to move to town and everyone knew each other by name. There was a public pool where kids went swimming, plenty of woods to run around, and several creeks streaming from the river, filled with salamanders and frogs.

For most young boys, it would have been heaven. But Billy preferred to stay inside and read about fantastic, faraway places on his computer tablet.

There was one story about the town that always stuck in his mind though. He'd heard it over and over again throughout his childhood. The rumor was that every full moon, the dead would rise from their graves and congregate in the town square, dancing and singing until the sun came up the next morning. A silly story, but Billy wanted to know if it was true. He begged and begged his parents to let him go see the Dance of the Dead, but they always refused. They said that it was strictly off-limits, especially to children.

"Even we aren't invited," they said. "It's a... special kind of party."

And so, during full moons, his parents always told him to "never, ever go to the center of town after dark." The local residents echoed the same sentiment. *Never.* They said. *Never ever go to the center of town when the moon is full.*

He'd always ask, "Why? Don't you want to know what really goes on?"

Their answers were unhelpful: "You don't want to know, Billy. Just trust me." They'd laugh it off and ruffle his hair.

But how bad could it be? Billy thought.

Some nights he'd lie awake in his bed imagining skeletons dancing from the verandas while confetti rained down in the moonlight. Eventually his curiosity got the best of him. The moon was high and bright, and after his parents went to sleep, Billy snuck out of bed. He tiptoed through the hall and down the stairs—avoiding the third step from the bottom which always creaked noisily. He'd done it. He was outside at nighttime, bathed in the light of the full moon.

There were no storm clouds gathered atop Tower Hill and the sky seemed to twinkle with more stars than he'd ever seen before. Billy watched in awe as a shooting star streaked overhead. It seemed to be pointing him towards the center of town.

The streets were quiet as he passed the darkened post office, the bank, the movie theater. He could hear music as he rounded the corner of State Street. The town square was lit with a bluish green light. A string band was playing on the steps of the Fountain House and the entire square was bustling with activity. The townspeople were all making merry, eating, drinking, and dancing, swaying side to side as they sang.

When the lighting strikes, high over town
Bolts of light in the night
When the lightning strikes, high over town

We all fall down!

Billy ran as fast as he could to join in the fun. Still in his pajamas, he circled around the center of town square taking in all the faces. A friendly-looking shaggy dog yelped at him and he bent down to pet it. The dog playfully nipped at his fingers, its mouth nearly toothless, its coat a dirty brown.

"And who might you be?" asked a kind voice behind him. Turning, he saw that the voice belonged to a tall, plump woman wearing a black bonnet and velvet tailcoat over a long and frilly pink dress. Billy looked around and noticed that everyone at the party wore old fashioned clothing, some of the styles reminding him of the drawing of Pilgrims he'd seen in a schoolbook. Billy felt silly in his somewhat worn blue pajamas, but he supposed the adults must be feeling pretty silly in their outfits, too. The Dance of the Dead must be some kind of costume party.

Billy immediately felt welcome. A heavyset man with long sideburns and a top hat handed him a large cup of ale and Billy sipped its foamy contents. Wiping his upper lip, he let out an excited squeal. This was everything he hoped it would be. Someone grabbed him by the arm, and he danced a jig around the square, singing along with a choir of voices.

When the lighting strikes, high over town
Bolts of light in the night
When the lightning strikes, high over town
We all fall down!

As the night wore on, Billy started to notice how strange the party truly was. Everyone's clothes were filthy, and their skin all seemed to be a greyish hue. On some, it was falling off in patches. Their crooning voices were unearthly. They were covered in mud like they'd just crawled out of their own graves, which they probably had. There were exposed bones and insects crawling on the moldering fabric of their garments. How much had these people spent on their costumes?

"What are you doing out here, boy?" a severe voice bellowed. Billy turned to find a man in a long coat of pale blue with golden trim. The jacket was missing several of its brass buttons and the stitching of the stars embroidered across his shoulders was frayed. The man grabbed hold of the neckline of Billy's pajamas with a filthy hand. Dirt was caked under his cracked fingernails. Billy looked up to see the torn skin of the man's neck. He only had one eye, the other was a gaping socket full of writhing worms!

Billy screamed and yanked himself out of the man's grip. The singing stopped all at once and people all turned to look at the young boy in the center of town square.

"What is it, Colonel?" a haggard voice called.

"It seems that a young boy has come to join us this full moon," the Colonel's voice rasped. The man knocked the dust from his wide brimmed hat as Billy looked up in horror. He was paralyzed with fear as the townspeople circled round, slowly sauntering towards him on decayed limbs.

Billy stood still as a statue as the dead all began to poke and prod him. They were intrigued by his pajamas, so immaculate compared to their filthy clothes. Even more so, they were interested in his soft, supple, living skin.

"What's he doing here?" one of them said.

"So tender, plump, and sweet," said another.

"Why, he even has all his hair!"

"Must have just passed."

"It's awful," a woman in the crowd cried. "What a terrible shame for such a young boy to be taken from the world."

I'm not dead, Billy wanted to say. But no words would escape his lips. His mouth worked soundlessly like a fish on dry land.

They wanted to know why he looked so... fresh. Billy was far too terrified to admit that he was still alive, especially not after the hospitality they'd shown him. Somehow it felt rude.

"I'm sorry I interrupted your party," he finally managed to say. "I had a fun time, but I have to be getting home now." He looked around at the sallow faces of the dead.

"Nonsense," they replied. "Stay and have fun with us. The streets are no place for a child at this time of night."

So, Billy stayed. The band struck up another tune and partygoers began once more to twirl and dance around town square. Billy tapped his foot to the music, nervously looking for a way to escape. Seeing his chance, he bolted towards State Street.

Just as he reached the corner, a familiar voice bellowed at his side. "Where do you think you're going, boy?"

Billy turned to see the Colonel sitting on a bench, his legs crossed, and a periodical in hand. "I have to get home, sir," Billy said, with a quiver.

"Nonsense," spoke the Colonel, patting the seat next to him, his joints crackling as he rapped on the wooden bench.

"I really..."

"I said, sit!" commanded the Colonel.

With a gulp Billy sat next to the decrepit corpse on the bench, trying not to look into his empty eye socket.

"Now tell me the truth, why did you come here tonight?" asked the Colonel.

"I've heard a lot about this, um, festival you have, and I wanted to see it for myself."

The officer nodded, watching the crowd with a smile. "That wasn't so hard, was it?"

"No, I guess not," Billy shuddered.

With his jawbone exposed, the Colonel offered a smile. "You remind me of my boy," he said. "He was around your age the last time I saw him." The Colonel stroked Billy's forehead with crooked bony fingers.

"What are you doing here?" Billy ventured to ask.

The old soldier shot him a surprised look, like he couldn't believe the audacity of the question. Billy shrank back, but he wanted to know why the dead were dancing in the town square.

"My name is Anthracite T. Campbell," began the man. "But you can call me Colonel. My tale is a heavy one, which I wouldn't want to burden one so young with." He hung his head as the woman in the pink dress approached the bench. She laid her bony hand on the Colonel's shoulder.

"Please, sir, I'd really like to know. I can handle it."

The Colonel glanced sadly at the lady in pink before he continued.

"I believe you've already met my daughter, Annabelle. Isn't she pretty?" Billy looked up at the woman's powdered face and clouded green eyes. "At least one of them came back to me," the Colonel continued. "The truth is, I shouldn't be here. Neither of us should be. It's a terrible fate that has befallen our family. I was a decorated soldier, climbing the Union ranks during the civil war."

"He was shot," added Annabelle, giving her father's shoulder a squeeze. "By one of his own men at the battle of Antietam."

"Your own troops?"

"No, by my superior officer," the Colonel scoffed. "General McClellan, the bastard. Shot me in the back of the head as I exited the officer's tent."

"Really?"

"I'm afraid so. Not sure who put him up to it. Probably the same rats who killed Lincoln. It's dirty business what they do down in that swamp they call the capital." The anger drained from the Colonel's mangled face and he nodded sadly. "They returned my mortal remains here to Boltsville, my hometown. For some time, I was happy. My wife and children would pick wildflowers from Tower Hill and lay them on my grave," the Colonel said, reaching up to take his daughter's hand. "It took out some of the sting of the betrayal I'd faced at Antietam. But after a few short years... they moved away."

"Really? Where'd they go?" asked Billy.

"Ohio," answered Annabelle.

"I've been coming up for the Dance of the Dead during full moons ever since. I'd like to believe that if my wife and son were to return, it would be enough, but I know it's not true. I'll never rest," the Colonel said, standing. "Not until I've had my sweet revenge on those who stole my life and my family from me!"

Billy looked to Annabelle with wide eyes. "Sheesh," he said. "What about you?"

She smiled at the boy, "It's another long and unhappy story," she said, as the music playing in town square changed from a slow song to a more energetic one. The partygoers yipped, dancing wildly, and clapping their hands. "Say, this is no time for talk of past hurts, not when the Dance is in full swing! Care to join me for a dance?"

Billy looked to the Colonel, who nodded at him encouragingly. Annabelle took the boy by his hand and the two ran to join the stomping crowd.

Billy laughed and danced with the dead all night, drinking their foamy ale and singing their forgotten songs until the first rays of dawn began peeking over the hills.

"Time to go," said one of the dead, as the dancing stopped. The crowd murmured, quietly saying their goodbyes. One by one the corpses ambled from the town square, back down towards the cemetery.

"Thank you everyone," Billy called out to the crowd. "I had a great time. I have to get home, but I hope to see you all next time."

"Nonsense," said Annabelle. "You've danced with the dead. You're one of us now. Come along, we wouldn't want you to get lost."

"Okay," Billy said, both confused and a little tipsy from the ale. He followed the crowd through town, stumbling as he went, until they reached the graveyard.

"Are we going to church?" asked Billy.

"No, we're going home," said the Colonel.

Phew! Home, Billy thought. He looked around at the headstones, the open graves, and mounds of dirt. Billy's stomach turned suddenly. "Wait," he protested. "This isn't my home."

"What do you mean?" asked Annabelle.

Billy watched in horror as several of the people just... sunk into open graves, sweeping the dirt back over themselves with their outstretched arms. They were returning to their "homes."

"Don't worry, Billy," assured the Colonel. "We'll find your home."

And so, as dawn continued to brighten, the dead set out to look for the boy's gravestone.

"But I don't have one!" said Billy. "I'm not dead."

"I know it's hard," Annabelle told the boy, stroking the top of his head. She took Billy by the hand and led him to a freshly dug grave as the sun continued to rise.

Billy eyed the horizon. If he could just hold out until morning... maybe he'd get out of this situation unscathed.

"Such an absolute shame," said Annabelle, shedding tears over an unmarked grave. "Not only to die so young, but without anyone to remember him. They didn't even engrave your name on the tombstone."

Billy struggled to loosen the woman's grasp. "Let go of me! I'm not going in there. It's not my home."

"If you won't return on your own, then we'll help you," Annabelle said, with a smile.

A crowd of corpses gathered round Billy, jostling and pushing him until he was standing at the edge of the opened hole.

"No!" Billy screamed. "Let go of me!"

"That's enough!" the Colonel yelled over the crowd. "Leave the boy alone. I'll take him home. Now go to bed, all of you." The Colonel stomped over to the grave and took Billy by the hand. "Hurry, the sun is nearly up!" he commanded.

"Thank you," Billy whimpered as the Colonel led him through the cemetery.

The Colonel took long strides, shielding his eyes from the sunlight before stopping near the cemetery's central mausoleum. At the Colonel's feet stood a large headstone, weathered and illegible.

"W-w-where are we going?" Billy said, his voice trembling.

"You're coming with me," the Colonel said, bending down.

"B-b-but I have to go home!" Billy said, tears streaming down his face.

"This is your home now," the Colonel said, pointing to his tombstone. "You remind me of my boy. He's never coming back, but at least, now, I'll have you to share eternity with."

"But I don't wanna," Billy blubbered.

"Think of all the fun we'll have dancing together under the full moon!"

Billy squeezed his eyes shut as the Colonel wrapped his arms around him. He could feel the dirt pouring over his body as the corpse's arms stiffened. He struggled against the embrace of death, swinging his limbs against the earth. Billy screamed.

The sun finally broke free from the tree line, casting warm light over the undisturbed graves of the Boltsville cemetery. The only sound to be heard was the birds chirping in the trees.

WE ALL FALL

Misused
    Mistrusted
Broken, beat, and lied to
Tied too
A life of limitations
Facing down the demons
Feeling kinda squeamish
Think we don't have feelings
Healing never happens
Hearts harden
Morals slacken
Trade it
Berate it
Bearer of the whip
Snaps
Collapse
Take another
Kill now
Breathing in
Never out

Greedy
Needy
Everyone had better please me
Tease me
Fake it
Take it
Try
You'll never make it
Burn sweet
The heat
Prickling on my skin
Stab me straight through
The monster I turned you into
A cycle the world can cling to
Darkening
Hardening
Our very existence
One by one
We all fall
We
All
F
.
A
.
.
L
.
.
.
L
.

12

LILIES OF THE FIELD

My sweet Annabelle,

I'm afraid I'm out of time. You've probably all but forgotten me, assumed me dead. Truth be told, I never thought I'd make it this long either. I wonder what you look like now. I hope that you are still as tender and kind as I remember you. I've enclosed a photograph of myself, assuming this letter reaches you. You'll probably find it hard to recognize my face behind the beard.

It's been twenty some odd years since I left that night. I'm sorry I didn't tell you I was leaving. I hoped the picnic we shared that afternoon would qualify as a proper goodbye. I've never let go of that memory, the two of us laying in the tall grass along the Ohio River. The riverbank was spotted with white and yellow lilies. A terrier ran along the water's edge, jumping up and down, yelping excitedly at the geese. We shared a cheese sandwich and sliced apple. You were whistling, trying your best to mimic the call of the chickadees, that twittered in the brush.

I lay on my side watching your curious eyes dart about the landscape as you spoke. You were wearing a paisley pink dress, like the one you wore at father's funeral. Such a beauty. The soft pink flesh of your lips puckering as you whistled. Your green eyes reflecting the afternoon sun. Each time you looked at me, your cheeks would dimple as you smiled.

That is how I will always remember you, a smiling curious girl in a pink dress, sitting on the bank of the Ohio.

I'm sure you were very lonely with only your cat and mother to talk to when I was gone. I'm sorry that I left you. There are many things I am sorry for.

When I left, I was young and brash, but not as clever as I thought myself to be. I assumed I'd find fortune and fame holding up rail cars like the cowboys I'd read about in the penny papers. I wanted glory, a glory I would never find in Ohio. I committed myself to a life of sin. I abandoned my family, those I loved most, and all of it for a thrill, a singular sensation.

I did many awful things during those early years out on the frontier, riding on horseback and by rail from shanty town to hell hole, from Sodom to Gomorrah. I learned every scheme under the sun as I drifted through the desperation and desolation. I robbed, cheated, and stole my way across the country. I did it without remorse. I did it to innocent hardworking people, decent people, who wanted nothing more than their own little piece of opportunity, enough prosperity to feed their burgeoning families.

I'd spend their stolen money on whiskey, and I drank until all the bottles were dry. I laid with whores. I gambled through the night, trembling with anticipation, my skin burning hot. Win or lose, I'd take my chances with lady luck until the sun rose again. I treated those who stood between me and a dollar like vermin. I'm not proud to say that I have killed many men: Indians, pioneers, gamblers, bandits, and lawmen. I watched from behind the barrel of my smoking gun as their bodies crumpled, blood pouring between their tensed fingers. I listened to their cries for help, for salvation, for rebirth, and I spat on their lifeless bodies when I was done.

Yes, I have been weak, and I have sinned.

Strangely, while living in the throes of this compulsion, I never once feared for my own life. The idea that I might die never crossed my mind, not until that day in the desert. There's nothing more terrifying than life without water, when all sensation is reduced to a single desire — an unquenchable thirst.

I'd met an oriental man, Kuru Kuru, in Virginia City, Nevada. He claimed to have information on a rail shipment. Not gold or silver, but bank notes. Enough of them, he claimed, to buy half of California. We agreed to split the haul. I'd put together the team of riders for the robbery, he'd supply the dynamite. If everything went as planned, we were to meet in Santa Fe to split the spoils.

On the day of the heist, myself and twenty other roughnecks hid along the tracks in the dim light of dawn. When we saw the plumes from the smokestack, we signaled ahead to Kuru Kuru and his men to blow the line. The blast went off just as the train passed us, sending lead, rail ties, and smoke into the air. The train's whistle sounded as the engine screeched to a halt. We came up quick behind it on horseback, rifles blazing.

It was a trap. There must have been a dozen U.S. Marshalls aboard — federales! There were other lawmen too, their deputies, even a gang of Apache mercenaries. We were outgunned and outmanned. We started taking fire through the slats of the iron cars. Then one of the train car doors swung open to reveal a howitzer. It blasted our left flank to pieces, sending our team scattering out into the desert hills. Buckshot grazed my left shoulder. I rode as fast as my horse would allow, watching as my men all fell from their own horses into the sand. Slaughtered, every one of them.

I was alone. I'd made it nearly five miles from the failed robbery before I saw the first rider tracking me from behind, then another, and another. Their dark silhouettes, high on horseback, clearly showed their drawn rifles as they gave chase.

After another hour of riding, much to my surprise, my gang of pursuers were not trying to close the distance. They'd flanked me on both sides and seemed content with just driving me deeper into the desert. I had only one choice, forward.

This continued for several more hours. By early afternoon, my water was gone. I kept tilting my canteen back, hopeful for one last drop. Blood was caked on my shoulder. The heat was sweltering. My throat grew dry, my horse's pace slowed. Still the marshals and their men kept at a distance.

We plodded forward, passing the exposed ribs of a fallen horse, picked clean and bleached white by the sun. There was nothing ahead but the sweltering sun, soft hills, and scrub brush. Behind us the shadows followed. I grew weak, delirious, and nearly fell from my horse several times. Then I saw it.

On the horizon an outcrop of black rock jutted up from the sand. I was heading straight for it. "Please let there be water," I muttered to myself, as my horse continued weakly forward. The object made no logical sense. It didn't belong in the landscape, and I started to think I was hallucinating. It looked like it had fallen from the sky, like a giant meteorite. The rock was black, smooth, and shiny. It appeared to have split into four pieces on impact. They looked like sharpened talons sticking out of the sand twenty feet in height.

When we reached the shade in between the four slabs of stone I dismounted. My horse collapsed from exhaustion into the sand. I stroked his long, dusty face. His neck was gaunt and his eyes wandered desperately. I considered putting him down. I looked back at the horizon where the horsemen waited, watching me.

I sat down beside my horse and leaned against the cool black stone. I don't know how to explain what happened next. With my head resting against the rock, time itself seemed to stop. I was no longer thirsty. I felt fresh, keen, and acute. I reached back to touch my wound. It was healed. I sat up with shock and looked off into the distance. The horsemen still sat on the horizon, but I could see them, their faces, the color of their clothes, the makes and positions of their guns. It was like I was looking through a telescope. I could see the star-shaped badge pinned to one of the men's chest, I could read the engraved lettering: U.S. Marshal.

I looked down at my horse, it blinked wanly taking shallow breaths. I don't know how, but I knew the truth, that this wasn't a random event. I had been chosen. The marshals weren't leading me to my death, I had been leading them to the stone. I also knew everything that would happen next, in exact detail.

I would touch the stone with one hand and my horse with the other, reviving my animal. It would stand as the marshals took aim at us. I'd lead the horse to safety behind one of the rocks as bullets began to fly. Shards of the black rock would shatter from the concussive force of the gunfire. I would sweep up as many of the fragments as possible from the sand before mounting my horse. We would ride, harder and faster than we ever had before. The horsemen would fire at us, but I would know the trajectories and speed of every bullet. I would easily evade their fire. The men would not follow me, they would stay with the stones. I would reach the safety of the Sierra Nevadas in three days time. I would start my life anew.

And that was exactly what happened.

When I reached San Francisco, I was a changed man. I knew I could not go back to the life I had been living. I had witnessed the work of a higher power. I knew that I could do good in the world. Immense good, and that I would be rewarded by God for my efforts. I, of course, also knew that the federal agent who had led me to the stone would continue searching for me.

Giving up my life of sin, I opened a general store under the alias Doc Baker. Keeping the stone fragments hidden in the lining of my clothes, I became a wealthy merchant and philanthropist. It was easy, almost effortless. I began by buying produce from the Central Valley for sale in my store using futures contracts. I always knew which harvests would be the best, which crops would fail, how much I'd be able to sell each season. I profited immensely, and I did it by feeding families.

Soon I had four stores, then twelve. My prices were always fair, often several percentage points cheaper than my competitors. I was accused of price fixing, of unethical practices. Attempts were made to sabotage my businesses, but I always saw them coming, zigging when they thought I'd zag. Soon Doc Baker's had locations up and down the coast.

Though successful, I placed large portions of my profits back into the local community, funding parks, museums, the arts, activities, and fairs. Anonymously, I paid for the construction of churches, a university, roads, cable cars, and affordable housing. There is no greater glory than the glory of God. I committed myself to doing his work and I did all that I could.

I married. Marianne is her name. Together we've had three children, two boys, Tobias and Clem, and one daughter, Annabelle. In them I have found a happiness and fulfillment that I never knew possible.

But I have reached the end of my line. Earlier this week while walking along the quay, I saw Kuru Kuru. He sat over a low fire, wearing a dark robe, and twirling the long white hairs of his mustache. He recognized me immediately. He looked up with his dark eyes and smiled, "Hell-woe."

I tipped my hat and strode away, but I know what seeing him means. The federal agents have found me. I will not escape them this time. I'm outnumbered and they have stones of their own. I don't know what they plan to do with me. I had hoped to leave the stones to my children, but they will not be safe with them. In three days, a package will arrive via one of my business contacts in Oregon. The package will contain all of the fragments I gathered in the desert that harrowing day. Keep them safe. Keep them in the family.

It's strange, for some reason I feel almost certain I knew this would happen. Like it was fate, predestined. I can't help but think that this has all happened before. That it will happen again. Until the cycle is broken.

By the time you receive this, I will in all likelihood be gone. I'm sorry that I missed so much of your life, and you mine. Be safe my sweet sister. The future is in your hands.

Your loving brother,
Deciduous Campbell

13

BETTER LEFT ALONE: PART 4

S heriff LeBuff sipped his coffee with one hand, steering with the other as the squad car climbed the steep hills. Deputy LeBlanc sat shotgun with his pointy knees nearly to his chin. He stared vacantly out the window. Mist rose from the blacktop of I-29; the sun shimmered at the horizon behind Tower Hill.

As the vehicle rounded the bend near where the tractor-trailer had lost control the previous night, LeBuff turned off the interstate, taking an exit ramp down into Devil's Gulch State Park and towards the river. From the high ridge they both watched the low clouds rolling through the valley below. Following the switchback, they descended into the fog.

"It's kind of dark down here," said LeBlanc. "Are you sure you don't want me to drive?"

Sheriff LeBuff rubbed his forehead, not wanting to take his eyes from the road. "Relax LeBlanc," he said. "Didn't you get enough driving in last night anyways?"

"What's that, sir?"

"I checked the odometer when I came in this morning. Where'd you get off to last night?"

"Oh, I couldn't sleep," the deputy shifted in his seat. "Just patrolled town for a couple of hours."

"What did I tell you about doing that?"

"Sorry sir."

"Have anything to report?"

"Nope."

"Right," said the sheriff, grimacing. He glanced over at his deputy in disbelief. Returning his gaze to the steep decline of rocky road ahead, he lifted his coffee to his lips as he hit a pothole. The squad car jerked forward, dislodging the lid from the sheriff's coffee cup. Hot liquid splashed across his lap.

Slamming the breaks, Sheriff LeBuff cursed loudly. Wanting to help his senior officer, Deputy LeBlanc attempted to pat the spill dry with his hands.

"Goddamn it, LeBlanc! Get your hands out of my crotch!"

"Sorry sir."

"For crying out loud."

After a few uncomfortable minutes, Sheriff LeBuff relinquished the brake and the squad car continued forward. Reaching the valley floor, the road finally flattened out, carving its way through the forest. LeBuff turned on the headlights, painting dark silhouettes of the trees through the dense fog.

They continued slowly on the poorly maintained road, towards the crash site. Ahead of them, pale blue lights circled in the fog.

"Oh god, not more ghosts," LeBuff said, grabbing his chest.

Concerned, Deputy LeBlanc squinted ahead as a black SUV came into view. It was blocking the road, low profile lights flashed atop the sleek vehicle.

"Oh, thank god," Sheriff LeBuff sighed.

"What is it, sir?"

"Looks like the FBI to me," answered the sheriff, stopping in front of the blockade, and shifting the car into park.

"What are they doing here?"

LeBuff stared down his deputy. "I don't know, LeBlanc. I guess I'll have to get out of the car and ask."

"Okay," answered LeBlanc, reaching for his door handle.

"You're staying here."

"Why?"

"'Cause I said so, that's why," the sheriff said, opening his door.

"Sir?"

"What is it!"

"Your pants."

LeBuff looked down at the stain on his crotch, "Shut up LeBlanc." The Sheriff slammed the door. The Deputy watched his senior officer start forward before turning back and reopening the door. "And no eavesdropping this time."

"What?"

The Sheriff leaned in towards the center console and turned on the radio. "I mean it," he said, cranking the knob to high. LeBuff slammed the door again and marched towards the black SUV.

A man Deputy LeBlanc didn't recognize exited the vehicle and met Sheriff LeBuff in the road. Deputy LeBlanc watched their lips closely as they talked, trying to capture as much of their conversation as possible. A twangy country song blared inside the squad car. LeBlanc leaned forward, he listened carefully.

14

SIREN RECORD

Flowers make no sound. Neither do paintings. Or, the old buildings in town. Unable to hear, it is always the smell of things that I remember. I am surprised I didn't smell what was coming that day my mother and I went inside the antique store on Sycamore Street. I was too busy looking for treasure buried between the stacks of misplaced and forgotten things to notice that hidden in the muddled fragrance of stale paper, dusty carpets, wood varnish, and mildew, something wicked was waiting for me.

The store clerk working that day should have been my first clue. She sat on a stool behind the front desk reading from a thick red ledger. The hairs on her jawline were longer than the ones atop my head. Gray and pointed, they curled off her flabby yellow chin.

An easily recognizable expression formed on her lips. "Good afternoon," she said. I was too busy staring at her hairy upper lip to get my mother's attention. "Hello? Ma'am?" she continued to say to my mom, who is also deaf. I pointed to my ears and shook my head. Her mouth formed a big oval and she nodded in understanding.

When I tapped my mother on the shoulder, she turned around to see the bearded clerk showing her crooked teeth in an apparent smile.

"Welcome!" the woman said, overdramatically shaping her lips as if we couldn't understand her. I rolled my eyes. My mom gave a dainty wave and clutched her notepad to her chest.

"Can I help you find anything today?" the woman continued, exposing the silver fillings and caps of her rotting teeth. I covered my nose as my mom scribbled a response on her pad of paper,

'*Not today, thank you.*'

"Big estate donation in the back left! Lots of new items." We both read from her lips. I signed *"thank you,"* touching my chin and extended my hand towards her.

I went straight to the estate items, passed the cubbies of furniture covered with ceramic figurines and cloudy glasses. There really wasn't much to see in the back-left corner of the antique shop. There were rows of glass milk bottles, a stuffed pheasant, and an odd assortment of wobbly furniture. Amongst the donated items I found a large cardboard box marked with the number nine. It was jammed full of old records. Rummaging through the collection, there was a surprising number of old jazz recordings. *Perfect!* My best friend Riley's father and my own father both had old record players, and Riley loved listening to jazz albums.

I ran to my mother, finding her holding up a lemonade pitcher to look at it in the light. She put it down and asked me, "What do you think?" with her hands.

"It's fine..." I signed.

"For grandma and grandpa's pool party next month," she smiled, finding justification for her purchase.

"It's great mom, but I found some cool jazz records. Can I get them?"

"That depends on who they're for and how much they cost?"

"They're really cheap! And Riley will love them." She shrugged with a dismissive acceptance and went back to admiring her pitcher.

Mom has always said there's nothing wrong with us. We were born this way. I don't often feel left out, but music is the one place where I sort of am. Often I read the lyrics, but I'm never super interested in musical artists. Still, I enjoy seeing the smile on Riley's face while he bobs his head to the sounds I will never hear.

I sorted through the 45 records, setting aside the ones I knew my best friend didn't have. There was a bunch by Duke Ellington, whoever he was. Then I found it, a rather strange looking album. It had no record sleeve, just a big red 'x' painted over its center. I set it aside in the purchase pile with the hope Riley or his brother would know it.

The almost-bearded lady gave me a weird look as I placed a stack of records on the desk. She counted the ten items at twenty-five cents apiece and marked it down in her ledger. Sliding the records back across the desk, I scooped them up in my arms. My mom got the pitcher and a lime green tray to match.

I pushed the door open with my hip and squinted into the afternoon sun. My ten-year-old sister, Julia, sat outside on a bench playing a videogame on her phone.

"How come Will got something?" Julia exclaimed upon seeing my haul.

"Because they were inexpensive, and he got them for Riley."

"You said we weren't allowed to get anything!"

"I did say that."

"Well, I want to go inside and find something."

"No, it's getting late."

"But—" My mom cut her off with a big wave of her hand and unlocked the car. My sister was such a brat. Julia didn't even come inside to help translate for me and mom.

I sat in the back seat of the car with the records on my lap while Julia and my mother argued up front. The unnamed record with the big red 'x' was on top of the stack. I shivered when I realized how much the symbol looked like it was painted with dried blood. As we pulled out of the parking lot, the sign of the shop with its faded yellow letters reading "Rustle County Relics" detached from one of its hinges and swayed ominously.

. . .

"Wow, thanks, man!" Riley signed, "These are great." Me, Riley, and Riley's brother Jake sat facing each other in their basement. The whole place looked the same as when it was first built: salmon-colored cushions, a great beige bar, and an old square TV set right into the wood paneling. With my haul of records spread across the floor, Riley and Jake were examining the album covers and track lists. The nameless red 'x' record stared at me from its place on the floor. It was there against the tan linoleum pulsing with magnetic energy. The more I stared, the more my heart began to beat faster. Jake saw me fixated on the disc.

"Will, what's this one?" Jake asked, facing me so I could read his lips as he reached across the pile and grabbed the anonymous record. Once it was in his hand, his skin rippled with goosebumps and all the hair on his arms stood up. I watched as Jake's eyes widened.

"I don't know," I replied. Riley translated my signs for his brother.

"Should we play it and see?" suggested Riley. Jake tilted his head, wary, but we were all curious to know what was on it.

"Allow me," I said grabbing the record and ignoring the foreboding tingle that shot up my arm. Riley sat excitedly hugging his knees. Jake tapped his fingers nervously. I placed the record on the turntable and hit the switch before setting the stylus in the 45's outermost grove. I watched it spin, stirring into a sickly red pool.

When I turned around, both Riley and his brother were standing up, rigid and emotionless. Their thick black eyelashes twitched and fluttered while their eyelids sagged at half-mast. Slowly, their heads began to lull backwards, and their eyes followed, rolling back into their heads. Then, all at once, their heads snapped forward and their eyes flew open with a newfound intensity.

Naively, I assumed the worst was over.

They sprang into action. Jake rounded the armchair in front of the TV and kicked it over. He leapt on top of it and, crouching like a feral cat, started clawing at the fabric with his nails. He dug so hard that his fingertips bled. I ran over to him and tried to push him away, but he punched me in the gut. I doubled over breathless, coughing as

I sputtered to the ground. I watched with terror as he started banging his head into the paneled walls.

Riley was in the same state of relentless destruction. Raging, he clawed at his chest, ripping his shirt and raking long, raw scratches into his skin. His lips stretched into a scream that I could not hear. I crawled over to him and got up to shake his shoulders. Looking into his glassy eyes, I knew he could not be reached.

Riley backhanded me viciously and I flew across the room, sliding along the floor into the corner. A look of shock that couldn't be smoothed away was plastered to my face. This was too much to be real. They were possessed by pure evil while I remained dangerously alone in my sanity.

I dared not stand and started to crawl back towards the record player where the untoward 45 spun and bubbled on the stand. Behind me, Riley and Jake were wrestling on the ground, punching, kicking, and hitting each other with all their might. A streak of blood splattered across the floor. Jake looked up at me from all fours, blood pooling beneath him. His nose lay crooked on his face, but he didn't seem to feel any pain.

Riley rolled away from his older brother and grabbed a cue stick off the wall. Riley swung it sideways with full force, hitting his brother in the ribs. I winced. I wanted to close my eyes, but my heart was racing with adrenaline.

Jake tackled Riley's legs and brought him down. They slid across the smooth surface of shuffleboard, all limbs and blurry fists. Seeing my chance, I crawled commando-style towards the record player, using the buffet to pull myself back up to my feet.

Riley toppled over the love seat and stumbled to the floor. He writhed spastically as Jake made his way behind the bar, grabbing a large glass liquor bottle. My hand shook as I fumbled at the switch trying to turn the record player off. As I flipped the switch, watching from the corner of my eye, Jake raised the heavy glass bottle over his head, preparing to bring it down on Riley's skull.

The record finally stopped spinning. Jake's arm went limp and the liquor bottle fell from his loosened grip. It shattered, sending brown liquor and shards of glass shards scattered across the floor. I saw Jake say "ouch" as he put his hand over his broken nose. Riley's jaw went slack, hanging wide open.

We all stood silent for a moment, trying to take in the scene.

"What the hell just happened?" Riley asked, looking down and rubbing the fresh scratches across his chest.

"It was the record. You both went mad when it started playing."

"This can't be real," Jake mumbled. Bewildered, I could barely read his lips.

"What was it playing?" I asked.

"I don't think I even remember hearing anything..." Riley started, "just a strange buzzing sound."

"A high, echoing note just going on and on and on..." Jake said, cupping his nose. With haunted eyes, his face twisted in agony. "It was terrible."

I looked down at the record in disgust. "Let's get some ice for your nose," I said.

"Oh my god," Riley looked on, dumbfounded. "Did I break his nose?" I simply nodded, brushing away the glass with my sneaker. "I seriously don't remember a thing."

"So, what now?" I asked, emphasizing 'now' with both my hands.

"We have to destroy it," Jake said, looking around at the mess they had — the record had — created in the basement. He stormed over to the sideboard, took the 45 off the player and, with two hands, brought it down over his knee. The record reverberated off without a dent. He tried again, this time over the corner of the sideboard. It didn't even make a scratch. Jake stared at it defeated then threw it as hard as he could onto the floor. It bounced and rolled along the linoleum flooring in a series of overlapping circles before finally coming to rest. The record remained in perfect condition, the red 'x' at its center gleaming in the overhead lights.

"I can't deal with this crap right now!" Jake yelled, slumping against the sideboard. He cupped his swollen nose.

"I'm sorry," Riley attempted to comfort his brother.

"Look at this place! Dad is going to be pissed."

The three of us didn't know what to do. We resigned to cleaning the basement, planning to reconvene the next night at my house. I took the record home with me. Since half of my family was deaf, we figured it was the safest place.

. . .

"What are you guys doing?" my sister asked the following afternoon as Riley, Jake, and I stood in the kitchen brainstorming ways to destroy the record.

"Nothing. Go away, Julia," I said, already annoyed.

Riley gave me a pointed look that said *We don't want her to get suspicious.* "We're just experimenting with the record your brother got me," he said, calmly.

"Is that the one from the antique shop?"

"Yes, now butt out! Go play with your dolls or something," I signed, angrily.

"I don't play with dolls anymore! Plus, Mom said you have to share."

"Go away."

"What's on it anyway?"

"Nothing," I replied.

"Can I listen?"

"It doesn't work," Jake added, with a dismissive shrug.

"Now, leave!" My sister crossed her arms and stomped away, the vibration of her heavy steps shooting up my legs as she retreated.

Then began a series of trials.

We tried drowning the record in the sink. It floated right back to the top. We tried smashing it with hammers. Then a sledgehammer. The thing was unbreakable. We lit it on fire in the driveway. Nothing. We covered it in lighter fluid and then lit it on fire. Still nothing.

After every attempt to destroy it, we went into my dad's office and played the record for just a second. Jake was too timid after his first encounter, he claimed he could still hear it echoing in his ears, so Riley volunteered. I'd drop the needle, waiting to see if Riley's eyes went glassy before turning it off and trying again to demolish the blasted thing. The last time, Riley lunged for my throat. Fortunately, I tripped backward, knocking the record player over and stopping the bewitching sound.

"That was close," I said, rubbing my throat as I tried to catch my breath. Riley tried to apologize but I wouldn't have it. It wasn't *really* his fault anyway.

"We've tried everything," I reasoned.

"I guess that means we have to hide it," Riley said.

"But where?"

The three of us watched a movie that night, waiting until it was dark enough to hide the record. Riley had a massive headache and said the grating sound of the record would not stop playing in his head.

Near midnight, we snuck out of the house, Riley still rubbing his temples. We walked behind my old childhood playset, with a shovel and the record in tow. We took turns digging for over an hour, until we were all convinced the hole was deep enough. We dropped the record in and began shoveling the earth back over it. Once we'd filled the hole, we covered the spot with a few branches and some leaves to disguise it. Dirty and exhausted, we prayed the next owners of the house would never decide to dig up the backyard.

We thought we had buried it for good.

. . .

After a paranoid month, our confidence grew that our plan had worked. Riley still complained of getting headaches too frequently for it to be normal and Jake couldn't shake that high lilting sound from his memory. But, as the end of the school year approached and summer began in earnest, we let it go, choosing to forget all about the terrible events that had transpired. It was gone. Finally, we could look forward to scouting trips, family vacation, and pool parties.

Every fourth of July, my mom and dad would throw a huge party at my grandparents' house. Everyone from the neighborhood would be invited, and this year's party was no different. Familiar faces, friends, and family swimming and playing lawn games. The grill was hot, and we were all eating, drinking, and being merry as the smell of burgers and dogs wafted in the summer air.

As was custom, my father had set up his old record player on the patio and connected it to the speaker system. He used the event as an excuse each year to dust off his old collection, and he and Riley's father were taking turns playing their favorite albums and talking about how everything sounded so much better on vinyl. I was thankful that the terrible record was buried three feet under in my backyard, several blocks away. Still, with records spinning on the patio my stomach turned at the thought of it. I tried to ignore the cold feeling in my gut as Riley and I passed the football to each other in the pool.

It was harder to ignore the ominous feeling when all the party-goers paused in unison. The football hit Riley in the face but he didn't even flinch as blood started to trickle from his nose. The ball floated beside him in the pool as his eyes glazed over, going white and distant. I watched, mortified, as everyone around me stood taught and rigid. It looked as if their backbones were all attached to a series of invisible strings that pulled them up. All at once they coiled backwards, their backs arched, their shoulder blades touching, their eyes rolling back in their heads, before springing into action.

Riley attacked the football like a rabid animal, squeezing and twisting it with both hands as he gnawed on the rawhide. Flattened, the ball hung limply in his mouth as he turned his gaze to me. He wasn't looking at me, he was looking through me, his wild eyes fixated on one thing — the urge to destroy. I knew *the* record must be playing.

I needed to get out of that pool. I swam as fast as I could to the ladder, forcing my arms to propel me forward. With every splash of chlorinated water my heart thundered in my chest. When I reached the first step, Riley grabbed hold of the back of my swim trunks. He yanked me backwards, pushing me down by my shoulders and forcing me underwater. Bubbles poured from my mouth, floating upwards, as I screamed. I kicked at Riley with my feet and swatted him away with my hands until I escaped his grasp. Reaching the ledge, I launched myself out of the pool.

I glanced over my shoulder, expecting Riley to be on my heels. He was still in the pool, seemingly content to slam the ladder against the side wall. He rattled and jerked it in wild spasms trying to break it free. Dripping and breathless, I looked across the pool to the patio where the record was spinning, untouched. Chaos unfolded around me. Hordes of people clawed at each other like savage fiends, digging into the lawn with their bare hands, punching, kicking, and screaming. Someone knocked the grill over. Charcoal burned in the grass while croquet balls, horseshoes, and hotdogs flew through the air. I needed to get to the record player before it was too late.

I made a break for it, crawling beneath the buffet table as Aunt Sally and Uncle Jim flailed beside me, choking each other and bashing their foreheads together. I sprang to my feet, ducking and dodging debris. Mrs. Jenkins hurled cans of soda into the pool before diving in and raking her face with her fingernails. Pieces of flesh floated around on the surface of the pool as the water swirled pink around her.

Cousin George appeared to be giving himself CPR as he lay poolside, pounding his chest and kicking his feet into the air. I jumped over him and grabbed a lawn chair. Using it as a shield, I plowed my way through the maddening crowd.

Sarah, a deaf girl from one of my classes, ran up the ramp to the pool shed as her girlfriends chased after her in a riot of pool noodles and kickboards. She was calling the police, a cellphone to her ear as she ran. I could only hope she remembered the emergency words they'd taught us in speech class for instances like this. Not that there'd ever been an instance like *this*.

Adrenaline pumped through my veins as I continued towards the record. My neighbor, Joe, was ripping grandma's flowers out from the bed and smashing them into his ears. Blood was pooling on the lawn as billows of gray smoke rose from the overturned grill. The scent was awful. And — holy crap — someone's hair was on fire! The stink of sweat, burnt hair, and the metallic smell of blood overpowered my senses. I stopped in my tracks and gagged.

I couldn't go on; I was frozen with terror.

The untoward record spun and spun and spun and spun, as a sanguine, rust colored liquid dripped down the sides of the record player. I covered my mouth and dropped to one knee, watching as my mother tried to protect herself with a pair of tongs beneath the patio table. I tried to sign to her, but I was shaking too badly.

Then, all at once, everyone stopped. I let out a brief sigh of relief, assuming someone had managed to turn the record off. Everyone dropped their makeshift weapons and turned towards the record player. *No.* They turned towards *me.*

Time froze. There was a new smell in the air, one of hopelessness. The toolshed was engulfed in flames. Sarah tried to escape through the small side window. Her mouth, stretched in torment, made the shape of the emergency word *"help."* My mother had knocked over the patio table and was swatting at Mrs. Riggins with tongs, as she lurched towards her. We were surrounded by the cursed listeners. They closed in around us with zombie-like movements and expressionless stares.

My body rocketed sideways as Riley tackled me. He knocked the wind out of me, and I lay on the ground gasping for air. Swinging my fist, I clocked Riley's jaw and he reeled back. He tripped me as I tried to get back up. A tray of overturned buns laid on the ground and I chucked them back at Riley as he crawled towards me.

I locked my eyes onto the record player, and in a last-ditch effort I dove towards it. The needle bounced across the record as it popped free of the turntable, fumbling onto the patio. People may assume that the deaf live in a soundless world, but I can assure you that not all quiet is created equal. The silence that surrounded me in that moment was the purest and most beautiful I have ever known.

I propped myself up on one elbow and looked behind me. Riley was slumped at my feet, tears streaming down his cheeks as he held his face in his hands. The scene of carnage and confusion that came into focus was in that moment a great relief. Exhausted, I rolled onto my back. I lay prone on the patio, the wooden slats hot beneath me. The sun shined overhead.

. . .

The police and paramedics arrived a few minutes later. The party was over, and this year's would not soon be forgotten. Nearly twenty people were carted off to the hospital. Fortunately, no one died. It turns out that it was my sister Julia who unearthed the album. She'd slipped it into my father's case of records the morning of the party. Her selfish curiosity only cost her a couple of broken ribs and fifteen stiches across her forehead. I told you she was a brat.

Aside from Mom, Sarah, and I, no one could remember a thing, just the faint memory of a song buzzing in their heads. Sheriff LeBuff nodded in disbelief as the three of us frantically signed to him what had happened. Much to my surprise, his deputy, Officer LeBlanc, was able to sign. I'd always heard strange stories about LeBlanc, that he was an emotionless cyborg, or a lanky athletic freak with no conscience, but he was nice. He listened carefully and helped each of us fill out our eyewitness accounts.

Sheriff LeBuff seemed less interested in our story. He kept to his duties, mostly cleaning up and helping to get people into the ambulance. I couldn't tell what he thought, if we were all crazy or delusional. He seemed completely unphased by the situation, like he'd seen this type of thing a thousand times. He continued his work, stopping occasionally to rub the white scruffy hairs of his chin with a quiet sadness in his eyes. He gathered our statements, promising to file a report, and took the record as evidence.

Not wanting something like this to ever happen again, Riley and I tugged on Sheriff LeBuff's sleeve. "What are you going to do with the record?" Riley asked.

The sheriff held the bagged record up with a concerned grimace. He said he'd keep it at the police station under lock and key. "This old thing will never see the light of day again," he promised.

We took Sheriff LeBuff at his word. We didn't really have a choice. Yet, I can't stop thinking about where the record came from and that big 'x' slashed on its front in the color of dried blood.

15

THE WEEPING SONG

Rain, rain, here to stay
    Children going to their graves
The Campbell's curse will come for all
Winter, Spring, Summer, Fall
Sally, Harold, Kate, Tyrone
Parents keep your children home
Gone to cinder, ash, and bone
Who will be the next to go?
Rain, rain here to stay
Children going to their graves

16

CHONG'S GARDEN

I took long, quick strides, scuffing the heels of my flats along the vacant walkways, as I made my way up the hill into campus. I'd spent all day cooped up in my apartment putting the finishing touches on my thesis. I must have lost track of time. I told Professor Beverly I'd have my paper to her by ten o'clock, and I had to hurry.

When I finally reached her office, I paused outside to catch my breath. After drinking nothing but coffee all day I felt nauseous and a bit faint. I took a deep breath, and gathering my courage entered through the open door.

Professor Beverly was at her desk, quietly reading from a large stack of papers by lamplight. She looked up at me and smiled with tired eyes. "Hello Miss Kirksguard," she said.

I tried to perk up for her, to look excited as I handed her my final paper. The truth was I didn't want it to be over. I loved being a student at Evermore College. I was good at it. I'd miss all of the time curled up in a blanket at the library reading from large tomes and writing papers. I had no idea what I was going to do after graduation.

She took my paper from me and traced the first few lines of the cover page with her eyes before returning her gaze to me. "So, I guess this it, Anna," she nodded.

I looked around her office, at the striped corduroy wallpaper, the crooked Jimmy Carter poster, and the dusty record player, remembering all the time I'd spent with her there.

"Yeah," I said. "I guess it is."

After we said our goodbyes, I walked back down the hill, overwhelmed by the realization that my college career had come to an end. I looked around the darkened campus with maudlin apprehension, trying to remember the excitement I felt my freshmen year. The walkways were well-lit, but empty. Everyone else had already gone home for the summer and I found the barren landscape both eerie and peaceful. The lights in the old brick buildings had all been turned off and, aside from the rhythmic sound of my footsteps, all I could hear were the leaves of the tall oak trees rustling overhead.

It wasn't until I reached the main drag that I realized I hadn't eaten all day. I scanned Main Street for a place to grab a bite, but all the storefronts, shops, and restaurants were already closed. The place was a ghost town. I needed to find something. There was nothing at my apartment but moving boxes, a typewriter, and my cat.

I stalked down the street for a couple of minutes, pondering my situation. The only restaurant with any lights on was Chong's Garden, a dingy little storefront popularly referred to as *Con's Den,* *The Den,* or just *Con's* because several of the lettered lights on the shop's sign had had burned out years ago. I'd never once eaten there during my four-year tenure at Evermore College.

I peered in through the greasy window, the red neon sign buzzing faintly within read: *Open!* Not seeing another option, I went inside. The bells overhead chimed, announcing my arrival.

The shop owner appeared to be cleaning up. He was a gaunt man, short and thin. His cotton t-shirt, marked with yellow stains, appeared to be completely soaked through with sweat. His head snapped back. "Hell-woe," he said, his eyes dark eyes narrowing into creases. He leaned the food tray he was carrying against his hip and wiped his forehead with his off hand. His thin mustache quivered with perspiration. "I be back." He smiled, revealing his crooked teeth, before exiting to the back.

I walked up to the display case, a fly circling my head. All of the food trays had already been removed, exposing the tracking for the gas lines beneath. Only the last tray, the one furthest from the window, was still sitting above its heating filament. It was *Today's Special*, labeled only as # 9.

The tiny man returned from the back. I looked at the *Vote Reagan* pin on the front of his shirt and frowned. He wiped his chin, returning my gaze. "Oh," he said. "Pretty eyes. Green like cat."

"Thanks."

"What you want?"

"It doesn't look like I have much choice," I said nodding at the remaining tray.

"Oh, you like. Very good. Very special."

I looked down at the contents of # 9, a dozen or so balls of meat smeared with a thick, coagulated, pink sauce. "What is it?"

"Oh, it cuddle fish meatball. Very good. Very special. I make just for you."

"Do you have anything else?"

He shook his head, "No, but I give all. Just for you. Special price."

I wasn't really sure I wanted it, but he was already spooning the contents of the tray into a Styrofoam to-go box. "Very good choice. Very good. Just for you." He walked over to the register, and I followed opposite him. He snapped a paper bag from beneath the counter and placed the Styrofoam box into it, adding napkins and plastic silverware. Then he reached under the counter again and winked at me.

From beneath counter he produced a single fortune cookie. He held it up and waved it in front of my face. "This fortune cookie," he said, dropping it into the bag. "Just words."

"This," he said, pointing to the Styrofoam container, "this your destiny." He punched the keys of the cash register and the machine came to life. *$0.99* flashed across the monitor. After I paid, he slid the paper bag across the counter to me.

"Hell-woe," he said, as the bells chimed overhead. "Come again."

I was glad to be out of there and back in the fresh air. Chong's smelled more like a zoo than a garden.

When I reached my apartment, I heard Meowlice Pawl, my cat, meowing. I locked the door behind me and made my way through the empty stillness to the living room where I put the paper bag down on a packing box. I looked around at the empty bookshelves, wishing they were still full, before pulling up a chair and unwrapping my *destiny*.

Meowlice snaked into the living room, dragging her black body against the doorframe as I sulked in front of my dinner. I didn't want to go back to Boltsville. I couldn't think of what possible future could be waiting for me there.

I nibbled on the fortune cookie, but it was stale. I was starving, so I ate it anyways. I picked out the fortune with an indifferent frown. *In the morning you will rise*, it read. I dropped the pointless piece of paper back into the bag and pushed open the Styrofoam container. I was still a little nervous about trying the food, but it didn't smell bad. Meowlice meowed curiously, pawing at my leg.

Using the plastic silverware, I cut a small piece from one of the meatballs. I put it in my mouth and chewed slowly, cautiously. The thick sauce was tart and creamy. It had an interesting flavor that I couldn't quite place. The meatball itself was surprisingly delicate, salty, and tender. After that my hunger took over, and before I could blink, I'd eaten four or five of the things. Meowlice continued to meow and paw at me, hoping I'd share.

While chewing the sixth meatball I noticed a strange texture in my mouth. I stopped chewing and felt around with my tongue. There was something in there, a wiry fiber or something. My mouth fell open.

I nearly gagged as I removed the Styrofoam container from my lap and placed it on the floor. I stood up with a disgusted grunt and strode to the bathroom. I spat into the sink, and wiped the saliva from my face, but I could still feel the filament tickling the back of my throat.

I went to the kitchen for a glass of water. It's just a piece of hair, I reassured myself, returning to the bathroom mirror. I took a sip of water, swished it around in my mouth and spat into the sink. I took another sip of water, repeating the process until the glass was empty. Still, I could feel the coarse fiber sticking there.

With a sigh, I leaned forward towards the mirror and opened my mouth. Taking my thumb and index fingers, I reached in and probed around. Locating the object, a thin wire, I was able to pinch it between my two fingers.

I started pulling at it, and it felt like I was pulling thread from a spool. I tilted my head back, my eyes widening with horror, as I exhumed a glistening black cord from the back of my throat. Mortified, I pulled until my arm reached full extension.

I tried to scream, but nothing came out. It was as if I were pulling out my own vocal cords. Tears began welling in my eyes. I moved frantically, spooling whatever it was around my finger and until my hand was once again at my mouth. I began to pull again, watching the mucousy cord grow in thickness and heft. My arm reached full extension again. The object appeared to have no end.

I heaved and whimpered as I spooled the mass once again around my hand until it was completely covered in a slimy black web. I tried pulling again, but now there was resistance. I could feel the thing dragging along the inside of my esophagus. Whatever it was, it was rooted deep inside of me. I tugged at it frantically, using my off hand and all my strength to pull. My cheeks glistened with tears as I continued to pull. I pulled until my mouth was stretched to its full width by the oozing tangle of black wire. I pulled and pulled until I was exhausted from the effort.

I slumped onto the sink, covered in sweat. I whined and mewled soundlessly, looking in the mirror at the slimy black rope that hung from my mouth. I began to weep, but my airways were clogged. Mucus shot from my nose as I gasped for air.

Think, Anna. Think...

Scissors. Get the scissors.

I stumbled out of the bathroom, dragging the weight of the black mass as I made my way to the living room. Meowlice lay motionless on her side in a puddle of pink ooze next to the Styrofoam container. I tried not to think about that, fumbling through the boxes until I found the scissors.

I staggered back to the bathroom dragging the black rope behind me, tracking goo across the kitchen floor and hallway. By now my whole body trembled as I stood before the mirror. I raised the scissors to my face. Opening the blades, I watched until they hovered outside the thick diameter of black cord. I closed my eyes and pressed down hard.

I yelped in pain. It felt like I'd cut into the flesh of my own tongue. I dropped the scissors to the floor, taking my free hand to my face and opening my eyes. Blood poured from where I'd cut into the black mass, dribbling down my chin. The thing writhed from my open mouth like a wounded animal, swinging my ensnared hand violently around the bathroom. Then suddenly it retracted. My trapped hand jerked forward punching me in the face. I fell to the floor, stunned.

Using my free hand, I braced my trapped arm against my body. Moaning, I rocked myself on the cool tiles, unsure of what to do. The thing, whatever it was, was trying to pull itself back inside of me. I fought against it, forcing myself back to my feet, but it was too strong. Supporting myself against the sink, I watched in horror as my hand was pulled into my open mouth. I couldn't fight it. Slowly my arm was dragged into my gaping orifice, nearly to my elbow. I could feel my hand inside my chest frantically grabbing around for something. It grabbed on and I could feel it, the beating of my own heart in my hand.

It started to pull again. Not in, but back out. I tried to stop it, struggling against the force with my off hand. I could feel my innards, unmoored, tearing away from inside of me. There was a popping sound and, looking into the mirror I watched my lips curl back, unfurling like a flower. My jaw unhinged as the hand dragged my pink fleshy insides out. Everything went black. The last thing I heard was the splat of my insides hitting the tile floor.

My insides out and my outsides in, I fell deep into myself. Falling, falling further and further into the vast darkness. I was drifting now, somewhere far away. Drifting in what I couldn't tell. It was something vast, nebulous, and completely alien to me. I felt warm, calm, and comfortable — as if I were floating in embryonic fluid, deep inside the womb of all creation.

It was dark, but I was moving. Drifting or floating. I couldn't tell if I was underwater or lost in space. Slowly, orbs of light began to flicker on in the distance, crackling with electricity as they came to life, one after another. Distantly, each burned with a pale light, resonant and buzzing like glass bells.

I continued to drift through the void, through the constant buzzing sound from the lighted orbs. In the distance a dark and massive object took form, spinning slowly towards me. As it grew nearer, I saw its features flashing in the light. It looked like a pagoda, tiered with seven levels, each one marked by protruding eaves. The lowest level was the widest and largest, with each subsequent level narrowing in a taper towards the top. Windowless, it appeared to be carved from a black stone, smoothed to a shine like onyx.

The object stopped spinning as it neared, and I could feel an energy pulling me towards it, and it towards me. I continued to drift in its direction, alighting atop the highest level, a rectangular plateau of smooth black stone. A tall pergola, or *torii*, stood before me — a vermillion gate, with tall pillars angled towards its upper lintel, an upturned arc of black stone.

At the center of the plateau was a short pedestal mounted with a fountain, or birdbath, carved of the same rock. The vibrations from the burning orbs of light intensified in frequency and pitch to a deafening shriek. The upturned arc at the top of the gate vibrated like a tuning fork. I looked around in all directions, nothingness dappled with burning balls of light. Then I walked through the gate.

The high-pitched ringing dropped to a low register, droning in deep distant waves. I walked towards the pedestal. Carved into the floor of the stone plateau were the words:

When the mind becomes focused

On things – yet to come
And Flows – ever so
Like a fountain
Trickling from its spout
Beware what lies beneath the surface
Deep in the cavernous basin
Debris, lingering and decayed
One should not drink the water
But, one must

THE WORDS READ FROM THE BOTTOM TO THE TOP, LEADING ME TOWARDS the fountain. A poem of sorts, written in the shape of a keyhole. I stepped atop the tiny platform cautiously. It felt like all of this had already happened, sometime long ago, before I was born. I peered at the contents of the fountain: black water. The surface began to ripple from its center as I drew closer. I could see the reflection of the humming orbs of light hanging overhead in the surface of the water. I placed my hands on the outer ring of the fountain and looked directly in.

Rushing water, starlight reflecting on its surface. Or was it the night sky? The silhouettes of two high ridges appeared along the periphery as I followed the sound of the water down. Down between the dark cliff faces to a teeming river that cut deep into the stone. I followed the snaking river, hovering above the surface where glimmers of starlight reflected in its peaks, valleys, and foam. I knew the place. Then, there along the side of the river, a fire burned in the darkness.

Four figures sat around the fire. I recognized one immediately. It was me. I was laughing and holding hands with the young man sitting next to me. The fire light drew his face from the shadows. It was Teddy Bridges, a boy I'd gone to high school with. *Teddy Bridges?* Across from us sat Rufus White, one of Teddy's friends. A young woman sat upon his lap that I didn't recognize. Then her name rang clearly in my mind, *Monica LeBuff*.

Teddy kissed me and I wrapped my arms around him. As he did, I could taste his saliva, feel my fingers running through his hair. The four of us were laughing and carrying on, but I couldn't hear what we were saying. All I could hear was the sound of rushing water. Then I looked into the fire.

The logs cracked and popped, engulfed in flame. From the base of the fire, where the coals burned hottest, the image of a baby appeared. It was sitting upright in a cloth diaper, its arms hanging towards its lap, its pudgy legs extended towards me. Looking up at me, the child smiled with gentle eyes. I wanted to hold it. I needed to hold it.

Drrrrrriiinnk! A voice called to me.

I could feel my hands digging into the rim of the fountain. It felt as if someone were pushing the back of my head towards the basin. I struggled against it as the voice continued to call.

Drrrrrriiinnk!

The sound of rushing water grew louder, the fire burned brighter, and the image of the child grew clearer. The baby's mouth curled upwards.

Drrrrrriiinnk!

It balled one of its tiny fists, squeezing.

Drrrrrriiinnk!

The expression on its face continued curling upwards, its brow furrowed into deep lines.

Drrrrrriiinnk!

It raised its balled fist, its eyes narrowed angrily, its mouth spreading open, exposing sharpened teeth.

Drrrrrriiinnk!

I struggled against it. The sound of rushing water was deafening.

Drrrrrriiinnk!

I sat up, gasping for air. I looked around, disoriented. I was in my bathroom, lying on the tile floor. I started to cough, struggling to breathe. My throat was hoarse and dry, my body covered in sweat. I ached all over and was too weak to stand. Nauseous and dehydrated, I crawled to the kitchen, my head pounding like a ringing bell.

From the kitchen I was able to see into the living room. Meowlice Pawl's body was curled and emaciated, lying in a dried puddle of black pus. I whimpered, desperately. It took all of my strength to pull my body up to the sink. Propping myself there, I turned on the faucet. I cupped my hands. I drank.

17

BETTER LEFT ALONE: PART 5

Sheriff LeBuff was still having a conversation with the federal agent while Deputy LeBlanc sat in the cruiser, leaning forward over his pointed knees, listening intently, and trying to read the officers' lips. A county song blared over the radio:

Oh, Anna. Oh, Anna.
You left me broken hearted.
I should have never started
Chase-ing Af-ter You.
Why-oh-you!

Sheriff LeBuff stood with his back to the cruiser, his thick knuckles resting on his hips. The federal agent appeared to be lecturing LeBuff, shaking his pointer finger vigorously as if in time with the music.

Oh, Anna...

LeBuff turned his head and spat as the federal agent finished what he was saying with a stern look. Behind the two men, the scene of the crash site was taking shape through the rising fog. The tractor-trailer was a pile of crumpled debris. The engine of the front cab was lodged into the ground. Its doors, dislodged and dented, lay atop piles of shattered glass. The wheels were scattered, some having rolled nearly to the river's edge. The trailer itself was a shell of twisted metal, torn in half at its center, its contents scattered across the forest floor.

A team of men dressed in hazmat coveralls with headlamps were shoveling the glowing gelatinous ooze into large containers. A heavily armored diesel truck rumbled in the distance as several more federal agents barked instructions into the morning air.

Sheriff LeBuff marched back to the squad car, biting his lip and slapping his hat across his legs. A dried coffee stain still showed on the crotch of his pants.

Deputy LeBlanc watched eagerly as his senior officer climbed back into the vehicle, slamming the driver's side door.

"What's going on?" asked LeBlanc.

"We're going back to the station," the sheriff answered, turning off the radio.

"What about..."

"What?" snarled the sheriff. "The shipment was to Belmont Asylum. It's a federal facility. It's out of our jurisdiction."

"Don't they at least want us to file a report?"

"What the hell do you think I was just doing, LeBlanc?"

"Oh, yeah," the deputy slunk back in his seat. "But, what's up with all the cephalopods?"

"The what?"

"The squids. Why were they shipping a tractor-trailer full of squid to the asylum? Why was the driver so scared last night? What is going on around here?"

"Stop," the sheriff said, dragging his hand across the deep creases of his forehead. "You can't ask so many questions." Sheriff LeBuff turned to his deputy, giving him a concerned look. "We have to be careful," he whispered. "Or, they'll come for us too."

"What? Who? What's going on?"

"Shh! I don't know," Sheriff LeBuff said, leaning back in his seat, exasperated. "What are they up to? Maybe they're putting something in the water. I have no idea. Whatever they're doing, it makes all the people around here crazy. But it don't matter, 'cause we can't touch them."

Deputy LeBlanc looked back to the crash site. The sun was burning the fog away as the team of federal workers continued to clean the goop from the forest floor.

"Stop staring, LeBlanc," the sheriff commanded. He shifted the squad car into reverse, jerking the wheel before shifting the car back into drive. He put his foot on the gas and the police cruiser sped away.

The two officers sat silent in the car as it climbed the hills out of the gulch towards I-29. Reaching a safe distance from the valley below, Sheriff LeBuff pulled to the side of the road and put the car in park.

"Over two hundred people have gone missing in Rustle County since I became sheriff," LeBuff said, staring blankly ahead, "There were more before that. Most of them children, but they range up in age as high as young adults. The innocent."

"What are we going to do?"

The sheriff turned and spoke sternly to his deputy. "You have one job, LeBlanc."

"What's that sir?"

"You gotta save the kids. You gotta try and save the kids," Sheriff LeBuff looked away, out over the valley and into the distance. "That's all we can do. Now go get 'em boy."

18

THE EYELASH WEAVER

There is nothing I wouldn't do for my baby sister Cassie. Ever since mom and dad brought her home from the hospital swaddled in a baby blanket, I've been her protector. Even though I'm four years her senior, she has always been my closest friend.

Things got harder after dad left. I wish I could say he got abducted by aliens or killed by one of the many spirits reported to haunt Rustle County. But I know the truth. I've stalked him on social media. Dad moved to Minnesota to live with some lady named Ruth. To keep up with the mortgage payments on the house, mom had to pick up extra shifts at the hospital, leaving me to have to take care of Cassie, mostly on my own.

It's not that I mind looking after my sister, most of the time anyway. She's not that bad. It's just been hard. We've both been dealing with dad leaving in our own ways. It makes Cassie sad, but mostly I get angry when I think about it. How could he leave us all alone? I know I shouldn't take my anger out on Cassie and I've tried not to. It's not always easy, though. I take after mom in looks, but Cassie is the spitting image of our father. She has the same flat nose and big brown eyes. I know it's not her fault. But, since he's been gone, sometimes just looking at Cassie makes me furious.

. . .

It was just a couple of weeks ago. Cassie and I were walking on one of the hiking trails, high along the ridge of Devil's Gulch. Cassie was getting on my last nerve. All morning she'd been pestering me to take her to the park, and now that I had she was "too hot" and "too tired." I need a break too sometimes, the chance to clear my mind, but she was being so clingy. My palm was soaked in sweat from having to hold her hand.

"I'm bored. Why did we have to come here?" She was driving me crazy with her endless whining. I only wanted to shut her up, just for a couple minutes.

Rustle County is a strange place. They say the old towers outside of town attract the unknown, the supernatural, that Satan himself swims in the Black Water River each night. Everyone around here has their own tall tale. With that in mind, and Cassie's constant complaints ringing in my ears, I decided it was time to spin a story of my very own.

I took Cassie by the hand and led her off the trail to a small clearing. We both sat down on a log, and Cassie sidled up next to me so close that our thighs were touching. It was mid-afternoon and the summer heat was stifling. I wiped the sweat from my forehead.

"I'm tired," Cassie whined. "Can we go home now?"

"We just got here."

"But I'm bored."

"That's why I'm going to tell you a story." Cassie tilted her head at me curiously while I tried to dream up something to entertain her. That was when I noticed a rogue eyelash lying on her freckled cheek. Using my pointer finger, I picked the eyelash off her cheek and held it up to her on the tip of my finger.

"Have you ever heard of the story of the Eyelash Weaver?" I asked.

Cassie shook her head no as she squinted into the sun. "What's an eyelash weaver?"

"There's a witch who lives in these woods," I said, trying to make my voice sound spooky. "They call her the Eyelash Weaver because if you lose an eyelash in these woods, she'll find it. And when she does, she'll take your eyelash back to her hobbled house on the knoll. Then using her magic and your eyelash, she'll cast a spell to unweave you. Stealing your youth so she can live on forever."

"Unweave?" Cassie asked, her brown eyes widening.

"Yeah, unweave. Like when you sew something together, only backwards."

"Uhm-uhm-uhm," Cassie mumbled. She reached tentatively for her eyelash, but I pulled my hand back.

"It starts with a faint tugging on your eyelashes. That's when you know you're in trouble." I raised my eyebrows and Cassie raised hers in pantomime. "She takes these hairs first," I said. "One by one, in a slow unweaving. Next," I stood. "Every hair is unstitched from your body! Then your fingertips. Then your toes. Until..." I trailed off. In my mind's eye, I could see it all so perfectly clear, the slow and terrible unwinding.

"Until what?" Cassie squirmed uncomfortably.

"Until there's nothing left of you," I whispered, taking the eyelash to my lips and blowing it into the air.

"No," Cassie screamed. She leapt, reaching up to try and catch the eyelash, but it was caught on the wind. We both watched as it drifted into the forest and out of sight. Cassie crossed her arms, pouting. "Why'd you do that?" she cried.

"Cass, relax. It was just a stupid joke. I was only trying to scare you."

My little sister looked up at me, her cheeks trembling as she wiped the tears from her eyes.

"I'm sorry," I reached out my hand. "Come on, let's go home." Cassie nodded, putting her hand in mine. We walked together along the winding trails, back towards our house. Cassie refused to look at me the whole way home.

. . .

"Dinner," I shouted, placing two bowls of mac and cheese on the kitchen table. I heard the TV click off and the sound of Cassie's footsteps as she shuffled down to the kitchen. She slunk into the chair across from me. She still wouldn't look at me. She just sat there sulking. She pushed the macaroni around with her fork, but wouldn't look up. I ignored her sullen mood, scarfing down my macaroni. It wasn't until I'd finished my dinner that I noticed Cassie still hadn't taken a bite.

"Eat," I said, pointing at her bowl.

"I'm not hungry."

"You know I made her up, right? There is no such thing as the Eyelash Weaver. Will you please just take a couple bites?"

Cassie prodded the mac and cheese, eyes downcast, before lifting the fork to her mouth. She took a small mouthful and chewed slowly.

"I'm tired," she said.

"Cass-"

"I'm just sleepy," she pouted. "Can I go to bed now?"

I nodded and took her uneaten dinner to the sink as Cassie stormed up the stairs. I tried to tell myself she'd feel better in the morning.

. . .

Feeling bad, I woke up early and made pancakes for breakfast, Cassie's favorite. It was my way of apologizing for being a jerk the day before.

"Cassie," I called up the stairs. "Your pancakes are getting cold."

It wasn't like Cassie to be late to breakfast, but I assumed she was still upset with me for scaring her. Cassie still hadn't come down to eat by the time I finished my breakfast. I sighed and jogged up the stairs to her bedroom door. I knocked.

"Go away!" Cassie yelled, through the door. I jiggled the handle, but it was locked.

"Cassie, let me in!"

I heard the soft creak of her weight crossing the floorboard, then a whimper as she unlocked the door. I pushed the door open, staring dumbfounded. Cassie had no eyelashes.

"What did you do!?" I scolded her. I felt sick to my stomach; I couldn't believe my little sister would take it this far. Cassie flopped onto her bed, burying her face.

"I didn't do it! She took them!" Cassie screamed into her pillow. Her body heaved as she began sobbing.

"Cass, I'm sorry I scared you." I sat down beside her, placing my hand on her shoulder. "But, you shouldn't do things like this just to get back at me." She grabbed a stuffed animal and chucked it at my head.

"Cassie-"

"Leave me alone. It's all your fault."

I sighed and retreated into the hall. I thought about calling mom, letting her know what Cassie had done, but she was under enough stress already. I went back downstairs, plopped myself on the couch in the living room, and turned on the TV. Everything would be okay, I told myself. When Cassie calmed down, we'd work it out.

I awoke on the couch with a strange uneasy feeling in my gut. I pulled my flip phone from my pocket and checked the time: 4:30 pm. I must have dozed off while watching TV. The house was quiet, and I found it strange that Cassie hadn't woken me up to make her something to eat. I headed upstairs to go check on her.

"Cass?" She didn't answer, so I pushed open her door. Cassie wasn't there. My heart thundered in my chest as my body filled with alarm and dread. "Cass?" I called, frantically searching from room to room. "Cassie!"

When I reached the bottom of the stairs, I noticed the front door was ajar. Our walk through the woods, the story, her sulking, her eyelashes, our argument, all of it replayed in my head. Cassie insisted the Eyelash Weaver was real. I threw on my sneakers and headed into the woods. Somehow, I knew she would be there.

Leaves crunched underfoot as I made my way hastily through the woods toward the clearing. I was looking down at my feet as I strode, trying to avoid tripping over tree roots, when I noticed a strange smell. It permeated the air, the scent of old bubble gum with the underlying hint of decay. The scent grew stronger as I walked. I felt sick to my stomach and had to stop. I placed my hand over my mouth and closed my eyes. I thought I might throw up. I took several slow breaths through my mouth until the feeling passed.

When I opened my eyes, a woman was standing right in front of me. I knew immediately that she was the source of the strange sickening smell. Her skin was pale grey and wrinkled. It hung loosely from her frame. She was a good head taller than me with straggly grey hair and cloudy eyes. She smiled at me, her grotesquely long eyelashes twitching erratically against her gaunt cheeks. I trembled at the sight of her, not just because she was terrifying, but because she looked exactly how I imagined her — *the Eyelash Weaver.*

She walked past me, ambling slowly, her long white lashes twitching frantically as she laid her eyes upon me. I gasped, afraid she would reach out and touch me. I squeezed my eyes closed and hid my face in my hands. It was only when I could no longer smell her putrid perfume that I was able to force my eyes open and continue looking for Cassie.

As I entered the clearing, I saw there was now a rounded knoll at its center. Upon it stood a rundown two-story brick house. Vines crawled up the side of the building, snaking in through the broken windows. The wooden front door sagged with age, hanging limply from its rusted hinges. I pushed the door open and peered into the darkness. I took a deep breath and walked inside.

Leaves crunched beneath my feet, cracking and splintered as I walked. I dared not look down. 'Leaves, I'm walking on leaves' I told myself, 'just old crunchy leaves.' I tried to imagine them beneath my feet, brown and crinkled, curling against themselves, the discarded leaves of autumn. I took slow, careful steps. Then my foot came down on something hard. It cracked beneath my weight. The sound reverberated through the room. I wasn't walking on leaves.

I looked down. The floor was littered with discolored bones. Maggots and worms squirmed beneath them on the dirt floor. I retched forward, doubling over, and tripped over a long femur. I fell to the ground, onto the scattered debris of death. My body shook as I pushed myself to all fours, heaving and panicked in the pale light of the room.

Gathering my courage, I stood, wiping my mouth with the back of my hand. I took a deep breath, continuing forward, one step, then another. Bones crunched to dust beneath my feet. I kept my gaze straight ahead. I had to find to find Cassie and get her out of here.

Reaching the stairs, I placed my hand on the banister. It was sticky, coated with, what I could only assume from the metallic scent in the air, half-dried blood. I didn't look. I put my foot on the first step. Bones crunched beneath me. The liquid from the banister coated my hand. "It's sweat. Your palms are just sweaty," I told myself, repeating the thought over and over in my head, trying to will myself forward. The banister slickened as I climbed higher, the blood growing fresher.

When I reached the landing, I felt lightheaded and I thought I might faint. "You're halfway there," I tried convincing myself. "The worst part is over." I let out a shaky breath, the twisting in my stomach began to subside. Then there was a loud bang as the front door swung open on its hinges. A tremor ran through me, and I felt my muscles tighten — her heady perfume preceded her like a bad omen.

"Who has been walking on my bones? "

Panicking, I tried to keep my breath even. I tried to think.

"Who has been retching on my bones?"

Fear seized me. I bolted up the stairs, knowing she would hear my feet thudding against the hardwood floor. I ran as fast as I could, over bones, and through dusty cobwebs, until I reached a door at the end of the hall. I turned the knob and hurried inside, slamming the door behind me. I looked anxiously around the room for something to use to jam the door. Then I saw her. The air rushed out of my lungs, and my body went limp. By the window, propped up in an old rocking chair, was Cassie — or what was left of Cassie. She was hairless from head to heel.

"Cassie," I called to her. She turned limply toward me, gripping the worn blanket that covered her frail body. My pupils dilated with growing horror as I noticed her fingertips were missing from her shaking hands. They'd already been unwoven. Her whole body was being weaved away, bit by precious bit.

"Cassie, we have to run!" She shook her head, throwing the blanket from her lap. I felt bile rising in my throat. Her legs ended in stumps just below the knee. She couldn't run; she couldn't even walk. Cassie looked back out the window, without emotion. She didn't speak, and I wondered if the Eyelash Weaver had already taken her vocal cords, her teeth, her tongue.

I heard a creak on the landing. The Weaver was biding her time, like a cat playing with its dinner. We had to go, and quick. I made myself move toward Cassie, afraid to touch her, afraid if I did, she might unravel completely. The floorboards in the hallway moaned. I hoisted Cassie up over my shoulder, ignoring how little she weighed, ignoring the stumps of her legs knocking against my torso.

"Just hold onto me Cassie, please." She said nothing in response, but I felt her stubby fingers curl around my shoulder.

The door flew open, the Weaver's ghastly figure stood in the archway. Biting down on my lip, I rushed at her, catching her off guard. Her bony fingers brushed against my arm, grasping for purchase but I pushed past her, knocking her to the floor as I barreled down the hall. Cassie's head bobbed against my shoulder as I ran. We were halfway down the stairs when my ankle rolled on a fragment of bone. I stumbled. Cassie flew from my grasp as we tumbled down the stairs.

I lay face down at the bottom of the stairs. I was dizzy. I could feel blood trickling from my elbow, where my skin was sliced open by a sharpened bone. Maggots and worms wriggled along my skin and in my hair. I rolled onto my back and looked up to the landing where the Eyelash Weaver stood. She held Cassie, curled like a deformed doll in her arms. She made a cooing noise as she brushed a finger across my little sister's cheek.

"Let her go." I protested, propping myself up into a sitting position. The Weaver clucked her tongue, her lashes flickered about her milky eyes.

"She is mine now. You gifted her to me when you let fly her eyelash in my wood." The Weaver smiled wickedly, showing her rotting teeth. I watched in horror as the Weaver waved her hand, and Cassie's fingers began to unweave. Her flesh, sinew, and bone came undone, disappearing into nothing.

"Please, please. Give her back. Make her whole again and give her back." My voice trembled.

"You ask me to give her up freely? To give back the youth I've gained from her?" The Waver sneered. Black ooze trickled from her mouth as she smiled. "Yet, you offer me nothing in return?"

I watched bleakly as Cassie's fingers shriveled down to her knuckles right before my eyes. My mouth felt incredibly dry, and I could barely choke out the words.

"What do you want? I'll give you anything if you weave her back together and let her go." Cassie's hands were little more than stubs at the wrist when the Eyelash Weaver snapped her fingers and the unweaving ceased. The most terrifying thing of all was watching the Weaver's sagging face curl into satisfied smile.

. . .

I turn back and look as Kaiden follows me along the hiking trail and into the woods.

"That is such bull," he says, popping another jellybean into his mouth and chomping it between his teeth. I shrug my shoulders, leaves crunching under our feet as I lead him into the clearing.

"I've met your little sister, you know. Her legs don't end in stumps, and she has eyelashes."

I turn to face him and take his hand, drawing my face close to his until our noses are almost touching. "I struck a deal with the Weaver to save my sister," I whisper.

Kaiden leans back and smirks at me. "Yeah right," he says.

"You don't believe me?"

"No."

"Then let me pluck one of your eyelashes," I say, placing my hand on his chest. "You're not scared, are you?"

Kaiden tilts his head skeptically, and sighs. "Of course not," he says, closing his eyes. "Go ahead."

I take my hand to his right eyelid and grasping a single hair, pluck it free.

"Ow," he grimaces, rubbing his eye. "Are you satisfied?"

I smile at him, raising the eyelash on the tip of my finger to my lips. I blow it into the wind.

"Yes, I'm satisfied."

THUNDERBIRD LANE

There's a low ridge of hills on the outskirts of Boltsville that sits between the town's center and Tower Hill. A dead-end street winds up along the ridge, lined with old dilapidated Victorian homes with wraparound front porches, gabled rooves, and brick chimneys. People in town refer to it as Thunderbird Lane. Named for the squawking sound the birds make when lighting strikes the towers. It used to be where all the wealthy people of Boltsville lived, before the brief mining boom puttered out. For the last fifty years it's been all but forgotten. Only brave children dare venture up the winding road.

It was a warm and muggy Friday night and the streetlights were dim and buzzing on Thunderbird Lane. Bugs swarmed around the bulbs of artificial light, in a constant search for whatever it is they're looking for in the thick night air.

Out of range of the streetlights, Dylan and Chaz knelt behind a row of overgrown hedges that lined the driveway of one of the rundown homes. It hadn't been occupied since the Braden family up and left town, right before Christmas. A wreath still hung on the front door, faded tinsel was wrapped around the railing of the front porch, and ornaments dangled from the empty branches of a dead Christmas tree that sat in the bay window.

"Did you bring the screwdriver?" Chaz asked.

"Yeah, it's the biggest one my dad had, but I can't lose it, or he'll kill me," Dylan said, sliding the tool out of his backpack.

Just then the two boys heard a sound start over the hissing cicadas.

"Someone's coming," Chaz whispered. The two boys dove into the hedges to hide.

A car slowly rolled up Thunderbird Lane with its headlights turned off. It stopped in front of the driveway of the abandoned Braden family home, only twenty feet from where Chaz and Dylan were hiding.

"It's..." Dylan started to say, but Chaz put his hand over his mouth, motioning for his friend to stay quiet. They both knew who it was, every kid knew who he was, Officer Craven LeBlanc, the sheriff's Dog, the Spook, the Cyborg. He was always showing up at random all over Rustle County. He patrolled through the nights, his silver eyes always watching.

Dylan attempted to get up, but Chaz grabbed his wrist. "Just shhh and don't move," Chaz whispered.

The spotlight of the police car turned on and angled towards the house. The cyborg opened his car door and, getting out, walked to the top of the driveway. The boys were frozen, their hearts racing as they held their breath. Officer LeBlanc stopped at the mailbox at the top of the driveway, 66 Thunderbird Lane. Both numbers had come loose and hung upside down appearing as nines. The Cyborg looked at the mailbox for a few moments, what seemed like an eternity to the boys.

Heat lightning crackled over Tower Hill. Birds squawked, swarming from out of the nearby bushes and trees. The sheriff's dog sniffed at the air several times as the birds darted about. He returned his attention to the mailbox. He flipped the overturned numbers back to their rightful places and walked back to his car. He climbed in through the open driver's side door, turned off the headlight, and drove away.

"What in the hell was that about?!" Dylan said, as he started to get up.

"Wait, stay down," whispered Chaz. "I see someone coming."

"I can't see crap. It's pitch friggin' dark."

"Shhhhut it," Chaz said, motioning for Dylan to get down. "Look," he pointed. There was someone coming down the block. It was a young girl, no more than 12 years old. She walked methodically, holding something in both hands that was hidden by the shadows.

She approached the driveway, rounding past the hedges, the heals of her red rhinestone shoes clicking on the blacktop. She walked right past the boys and disappeared behind the old Braden family home.

"What is she doing here?" Dylan asked.

"Shh," Chaz instructed. Both boys listened. They heard what sounded like the backdoor of the house creaking open, then the screen door slammed shut.

"Let's get out of here," Dylan said. "This is totally stupid!"

"Oh, come on man, it's just starting to get fun," Chaz said, grabbing Dylan by the arm and pulling him through the hedges.

The two boys crept onto the front porch. They looked in through the bay window. It was hard to see anything with the Christmas tree blocking their view. There was a light on in one of the downstairs rooms, casting a soft light down the darkened hallway.

"Let's go around the back," Chaz whispered.

"Dude, can we just get outta here, like now?" Dylan replied.

"Seriously? You half sissy. You're afraid of a little girl?"

Dylan crossed his arms and sighed. "Fine," he said. "Let's just get it over with already."

THEY MADE THEIR WAY AROUND TO THE BACK OF THE HOUSE, PASSING the long sideboards of peeling paint. Behind the house there was a concrete stoop that led up to the back door. They climbed the concrete steps. The backdoor was open, the rusty screen door shut. Chaz quietly turned the doorknob to see if it was unlocked. It was. He looked at Dylan and put his fingers to his lips, signaling him to stay quiet and follow him into the house.

They entered through the kitchen; its walls lined with antique-looking cabinets of dark varnished wood. Off to the left was the living room with the dead Christmas tree standing in the window. A light came from an open door down the hall. There was a sheet, or some kind of bath towel, draped across the doorway making it hard to see if anyone or anything was in the dimly lit room.

"There's still presents. Look. Under the tree. Dude. Jackpot!" whispered Chaz. "I told you."

Dylan stared down the hallway at the light coming from the edges of the open doorway. He looked over at the stack of boxes under the Christmas tree. "What do you want me to do?" he asked.

Chaz had it figured out. "I'll watch the doors. You go open the presents, see if there's anything good."

Dylan hesitated. "It smells like fried calamari in here..."

"Just go!" Chaz whispered, pushing Dylan in the direction of the living room.

Dylan walked carefully into the living room, the floorboards squeaking beneath his feet. He picked up one of the boxes and the wrapping paper rustled.

"Shh," Chaz warned.

"Sorry," Dylan mumbled. It wasn't humanly possible to even touch the presents without making a racket. He took the screwdriver out from his backpack and felt around the box for a loose piece of tape. He figured by cutting the tape he might be able to slide the gift out. Making as little noise as possible, he fumbled around with the present, before finally managing to remove the wrapping paper.

"What the hell is this?" Dylan said, as he inspected the object. Only the faintest bit of streetlight was passing through the bay window, and he could hardly see. "It looks like an empty box of macaroni." He straightened to see what the object was, but he was dumbfounded. "What?" He looked back to Chaz, but his friend was gone.

"Chaz," Dylan whispered. "Chaz!" a bit louder. Dylan put the box down and looked around. His heart was racing. He tiptoed towards the kitchen. A dim light glowed at the far end of the hall. Where the hell was Chaz? He was just standing right here.

Dylan peeked around the corner and down the hallway. The silhouette of a small girl was cast upon the sheet that covered the doorway at the end of the hall. Dylan was frozen, his feet heavy as cement, his heart beating a mile a minute in his chest. He made a break for the backdoor but tripped over something and fell to the kitchen floor. He looked to see Chaz lying face down in a puddle of blood.

Dylan screamed, rolling over and pushing himself back up to his feet. He looked to the backdoor. The little girl was standing in front of it, wearing a dress of pink and white cotton with her hands behind her back. Her head was down so that her dark bangs covered her face.

"Teehee," she laughed, brushing the hair away from her face. Her eyes glowed a demonic red as she exposed the blood-soaked knife in her other hand.

"Chaaaaz!" Dylan screamed, leaping out of the way to avoid the girl's swinging blade. It grazed his hip as he turned and ran to the living room, screaming the whole way.

He reached the front door and fumbled trying to get it open as the girl bounded towards him, swiping at him with her knife.

"Oww, stop!" Dylan yelled. He felt a burning sensation as the blade sliced across his shoulder blade. Dylan turned and put his hands up, shouting, "Why!? What do you want?" The girl sliced his outstretched palms. He dropped to his knees and started crying, still holding his hands up to protect his face. "Why are you doing this?"

The girl stood over him, wiping the knife along her cotton dress. "Because," she hissed. "Someone else needs your life." She parted her dark hair, exposing her pale grin. "And they need it now."

Headlights flashed in through the bay window. The little girl shielded her face from the light and Dylan sprang to his feet. He pushed her over and sprinted towards the backdoor. He didn't stop to open it. He dove straight through it, shattering the window. Shards of glass tinkled atop the concrete stoop as he landed hard in the grass of the backyard.

The wind was knocked out of him, but he scrambled to all fours, bloody and gasping for air. A hand grabbed his shoulder. He looked back, his eyes brimming with terror. "Noooo!"

It was Officer LeBlanc, his silver eyes shining. Lightning flashed overhead as the officer drew his gun.

"Don't go in there," Dylan mumbled, slumping back into the grass.

Officer LeBlanc ran into the house. After performing a full sweep, he found it was empty. Dylan tried to explain to him what had happened, but the details didn't add up. There was no Christmas tree in the window, no presents, no little girl, no blood, no knife, no Chaz, nothing. Just a dirty old mattress in the room at the end of the hall, encircled by a shrine of melted wax.

Dylan was paranoid, and it looked like the cuts on his body might have come from jumping through the window. He was hysterical, but if LeBlanc thought he was crazy, the officer didn't show it. He showed no emotion at all. He just nodded, asked questions, and drove the boy to the hospital.

A few days later, Chaz's parents filed a missing persons report with the County Police, a futile effort. Chaz was gone. Dylan might have been too. Never would he return to the old winding road outside of town, with its Victorian homes, the wraparound porches, the gabled rooves, and brick chimneys. He would never go back to Thunderbird Lane.

20

BETTER LEFT ALONE: PART 6

A car door slammed shut. Sheriff LeBuff sat up in his seat, the crumpled plastic wrappers of pastries falling from his lap to his feet. It wasn't just his eyes that were glazed, his mouth was too.

He wiped his face, listening as the sharp clicking of heels pealed into the night. As the sound trailed off, he looked through the passenger side window. The beam of a flashlight bobbed from side to side in the distance, divided by the narrow silhouette of his deputy. He watched until the bouncing light disappeared into the night.

"That a boy," he said.

He turned the radio on, the volume low. A sad old country song played.

"That a boy," he said again, rubbing his knees. "This old dog is too tired for the chase."

A long high note of lament played on the radio.

"You get 'em boy. You get 'em all," the sheriff said, staring off into the night. He listened until the song had ended before starting the police car. He turned off the radio and drove around town, the windows down, just listening to the night. The streets were empty. They were always empty.

Sheriff LeBuff stopped at the intersection of East Street and

Belmont Avenue. He shifted the car into park. He looked over at the towering concrete building, its windows shuttered and barred. A perimeter of electrical fence, topped with razor wire, circled the compound. The building was shrouded in darkness. A single light burned at the front gate above a sign that read: *Belmont Asylum. Private Property. No Trespassing.*

"I'm still looking, Monica," the sheriff whispered to himself. "I haven't given up. Not yet. Not after all these years. I promised mother I'd find you, and I will."

Sheriff LeBuff took off his hat and stroked his thinning hair. The mounted cameras outside the asylum were all watching him, and he knew it. He bowed his head and looked over at the darkened building. "You in there?" he asked. "If you are, you go ahead and give me the sign. I'll come in and get you out of there."

Sheriff LeBuff stared at the barred windows of the asylum for several long minutes, the fence, the razor wire. Crickets chirped. He looked up to Tower Hill, where lightning flickered in the night.

21

A LOSING GAME

Colin was a friend of mine. The two of us bonded in middle school. We both came from what I guess you'd call troubled families. His parents divorced shortly after he was born. His mom and dad remarried after that. He was lost in the middle somewhere, the forgotten child. No one cared about Colin. No one, except me.

My family was another story. I'm sure my parents loved each other. I'm sure they loved me, but the constant fighting was more than I could stand. Each night Colin and I would meet up to hang out, me trying to escape my family, him without one at all. We were the unwanted.

Kids like us always get the short end of the stick. Even when we do the right thing. If no one is going to trust or believe in you, what's the point? Instead of trying to fit in, Colin and I rebelled. We'd stay out all night, just the two of us, playing ding-dong-ditch, shoplifting candy and lighters from the convenience store, listening to the radio, and stealing lawn ornaments out of people's yards. We didn't mean anything by it. It was just for fun. It sure beat going home.

One night, Colin talked me into breaking into the arcade with him after dark. Neither of us could afford to play the games inside, so I didn't require much convincing.

He told me he knew a secret way to get in. I didn't think he was serious until we were already halfway up the escape ladder out back. There was a loose vent cover on the roof. We climbed right in.

As we crawled through the cramped ventilation ducts, I asked him, "How'd you find out about this place?" He said he heard about it from some ninth graders. Part of me suspected he found it himself.

When we climbed out of the ducts, the arcade was dark. Games stood in rows all around us, blank and vacant.

"Whoa," I said, looking at Colin.

He just smiled, "Come on. I want to show you something."

I was surprised when Colin didn't stop to power up any of the games. Instead he led me right to the back of the arcade, to a door labeled: *Employees Only.*

"Wait till you see this," he said, pushing open the door.

Inside there was just a bunch of out-of-order games. I was annoyed we were back here with this junk when all the cool games were up front. Neither of us had our own game console. We were missing our chance. Colin didn't seem to think so, he walked up to a dusty old pinball machine like he'd been waiting his whole life to play it.

"Dude?" I said, kicking the leg of the rusty machine. "What are we doing back here?" Colin winked at me. He pulled a silver dollar out of his pocket dropped it into the dingy coin slot.

"What'd you do that for?" I shouted. I couldn't believe he'd waste a whole dollar on some crappy game. Then, with a yank of his fingers Colin pulled the silver coin back out of the slot. It hung by a string in front of his widening grin.

"I thought you knew me better than that, Grant."

The pinball machine sparked to life, lights flashed, and electronic music played. I didn't want to embarrass myself by second-guessing Colin again, but I didn't think he brought me here just to play some bumpers.

Before I could complain, the floor beneath the machine started to spin, rotating until a hidden door appeared on the wall behind the game. A hazy green light emanated from the open door. Colin didn't waste any time, he walked right inside. I was confused, but with my curiosity piqued, I followed close behind.

In the center of the dark room a glowing green sphere hovered at chest-height. The object pulsed from dim to bright, as if breathing. Colin approached and the sphere brightened into a solid electrical green. It chimed pleasantly, like it was greeting him. I circled the object, trying to make sense of it. It was floating in midair with no base to hold it up. It looked like it came from another planet.

Turning to Colin, I asked, "What is this thing?"

"You'll see."

"Who did you hear about this from, again?"

"Johnny, Tommy, and Derek."

"Wait," I said, giving Colin a look. "Aren't they all missing?" I was right. No one had seen those boys for two weeks. It was in the newspaper and everything.

"Kind of," Colin said, looking down at his wrist. "If you're scared, you don't have to do it." Colin placed his hand on the sphere. Its luminescent surface reacted to his touch, rippling in waves around his fingers. A deep purring sound came from the orb as Colin's face stretched into a smile.

He closed his eyes and took a deep breath as the orb radiated with bright light. Its green energy crawled up his hand, quickly consuming his whole arm. I jumped back in shock, but Colin kept smiling. The glowing green light shot down the length of his body, pulsing as it consumed him. As the green energy reached his face, he winked at me and said, "Dude, you're going to love this."

In a flash the emerald energy returned to the sphere, Colin with it. He'd disappeared into thin air! The orb floated in the center of the room, chiming as it returned to a solid green.

"Colin!" I called. "Colin?" I wasn't sure what to do. I wondered if I should just wait for him to come back. I didn't want to be chicken and run home.

I stepped toward the object, whatever-it-was. Following Colin's actions, I placed my hand onto the bright green surface. It purred and rippled in response to my touch. It vibrated gently, smooth and warm under my skin. It didn't just feel warm, it filled me with warmth. My veins pulsed, tingling with a sensation that nearly brought me to laughter. I didn't know what it was, but it felt great.

It stopped and asked me if this is what I wanted. I don't know exactly how it asked because there weren't any words, but I felt an invitation presented and gladly accepted.

Then there was not only warmth, but radiant joy coursing through my chest. The orb grew blindingly bright as its energy seeped into my skin. Green light engulfed my arm and with it, ecstasy flowed into my body. It felt amazing, like everything I'd ever wanted. White light flooded my vision and I let go of all my wants and desires.

My pupils yawned spastically as they adjusted to the saturation of light. Slowly, it came into view. I was standing in a vast field of tall flowing grass. Snow-capped mountains draped the horizon. The sun shimmered behind them, casting dramatic shadows across the sloping landscape. Rays of light danced across the dewy grass. Rainbows of refracted light glimmered in the dew. It all seemed too fantastic to be real. I was astounded. It was spectacular.

I spotted Colin darting through the grass below. Running faster than I knew possible. His physical body was somehow changed, no longer chubby, he was tall and athletic. His bulging biceps pumped at his sides as he ran.

He waved to me, dashing effortlessly through the tall grass of the valley. When I waved back, I noticed something on my wrist. It was a rectangular screen, the width of my forearm, but I could see through it like a hologram. On the screen, Colin's face projected as he spoke in real time.

"Follow me this way!" the sound of his voice was clear inside my head.

"How?" I asked, unsure of how he could reach such speeds.

"Just go. You can do it."

I shook my head, "How?"

He stopped and zoomed back to me in a blur. He stood in front of me almost instantly. With a nod, he pointed to the module on his wrist and showed me how to change my personal settings.

"Everything is done telepathically," he instructed. "Just think it and it happens."

I held my own wrist module up, using it as a mirror as I altered my body. I picked a tall lean frame for myself. Colin approved with a thumbs up. On a whim, I gave myself a pink mohawk.

"Nice," Colin remarked. He looked at his watch device and gave himself fire-red hair, styled into spikes.

"I think I'm getting the hang of this," I said.

He told me to do the same thing if I wanted to run fast. Just think it.

"Try to keep up," he said. I watched as he sprinted through the swaying grass. I willed myself forward. I was surprised at how easily my body kept pace with Colin. He saw that I was at his heels and accelerated, shooting ahead.

With a grin, I leapt into the air and took flight above his head. I whizzed past him at breakneck speed.

"This is awesome!"

"Now you're getting it," he said, springing into the air behind me. He rocketed towards me and we both stopped in midair, hovering high above the valley.

"How many times have you done this?" I asked.

"Just once," he said. "Check this out."

I followed him as we flew over the grasslands, towards the sea. We passed over the edge of a cliff, towering miles above the shimmering water. From below, a massive serpent swooped up after us. We both dodged as its fearsome jaws snapped at us. I froze in awe, watching as its long, scaled body glided by me.

"Whoa."

Colin smirked and held up his hand, curling his fingers into a ball. A flame ignited, raging in his hand.

"Whoa," I said again, unable to think of any other words.

He pulled back his fist and swung it forward, unleashing a hailstorm of fireballs at the coiling dragon. They exploded as they crashed against the creature's back with utter realism.

The beast wailed a thunderous roar and turned toward us. It flew in our direction. Colin tried to beat it back, lobbing fistfuls of fire, but the creature was undeterred. It barreled forward, taking hits to the face. Its rabid jaw swung open, and Colin bolted out of the way.

I held my ground as the dragon continued towards me. I forcefully held out my hands, creating a large plasma shield in front of me. The creature rammed into it headfirst, going full speed. It crumpled against the immovable force. Critically dazed, the beast fell from the sky.

"Alright, Grant!" Colin cheered. He rained destruction down onto the plummeting serpent and I dove after it, cutting through the air with precision. At my command, a neon spectral sword materialized in my hand. I slashed into the tumbling beast, cutting through its heart with my glowing sword. All I had to do was think it and it happened. It was as simple as that. The power I felt was irresistible. I watched as the dragon's lifeless body crashed into the sea below me. In the distance a lightning storm raged over the ocean.

"Wow, that was awesome," Colin said, zipping to my side. "I've never seen it killed like that."

"It was pretty cool."

"I know, right?" he chuckled.

"What would have happened if it got me?" I asked.

"Nothing," he answered. "You just end up back in the field."

"So, you can't die here?"

"No, you can't die," he said, hesitating. He looked off to the distant storm. "But other things can happen."

"Like what?" I questioned, but before he could answer, another voice spoke clearly in my mind.

"Colin!" It took a moment for me recognize his voice, but it was Derek, one of the missing ninth graders. The whole town had been looking for him for weeks. I turned to see him standing on the cliff's edge. He looked much older with white hair and a long wispy beard. His dark eyes peered out from beneath the hood of his blue robe.

"He can be saved," Derek bellowed.

Wind whipped at my face as I looked to Colin. "Who's he talking about?" I asked.

"Tommy," Colin said, pointing to the distant storm.

"Tommy is in that storm cloud?" I asked.

Colin's eyes saddened. "That is Tommy now," he replied.

We both stared at the billowing clouds and crackling lightning as Derek flew to meet us.

"I can still contact him," Derek said, holding up his wrist. Tommy's profile displayed on the screen. It was nothing but static. "The reception's bad, but he's still in there." Derek put down his hand and bowed his head. "Johnny, on the other hand, he's gone now."

"I thought you said we couldn't die." I shot Colin a look.

"Yeah, that's what I said."

The prospect that I could be lost in this place sent panic racing through my heart.

"Colin, I want to leave. Now," I said.

"Alright," he threw his hands up. "I'll get you out of here."

"Tommy doesn't have much time," Derek warned. "I need your help to get him back."

"Let me get Grant out of here and then I'll come back to help you," Colin said. Derek nodded and took off, his robe thrashing behind him.

Colin turned back to me. "Put your right hand out, like you had it on the sphere," he said, grabbing my hand and putting it in place for me. "Put your left hand on your heart and close your eyes."

I nodded, hand on my chest, and squeezed my eyelids shut. When I opened them, I stood in the small dark room again, hand resting on the vibrating orb. I stumbled backward, falling away from the sphere as it returned to a solid green.

My heart was racing, I could hardly breathe. I wanted to escape into the night air, but I waited for Colin. He materialized before me in a flash of emerald light.

"What is this thing?" I asked, panting.

"I don't know," he said, looking into the bright green light of the orb. "Didn't you like it? It was fun, right?" I squinted at him skeptically as he continued. "I mean, as long as you don't lose yourself in there — it's great. Have you ever felt that powerful? In your whole life, have you ever felt better than that?"

"How did Tommy lose himself in there anyway?" I asked. "He's turned into a bunch of storm clouds? How'd that happen?"

"C'mon, don't act like you didn't feel it in there. All of us want to escape," he said. "Some of us more than others."

"But why would he let that happen to himself?" I asked

"Tommy's not gone. You don't understand. He's a god now. A force of nature. He's finally free," he said. "Being in there," he held his thought as he stared into the orb's radiant light. "There's nothing else like it."

"You're going back?" I asked, as Colin turned and put his hand on the sphere.

"I have to," he said. Green light engulfed him again, and he was gone.

I left the arcade the way I came in. I was happy to finally get back outside. Stars hung overhead and crickets chirped as I walked home beneath the streetlights. That's when I noticed the holographic module was still attached to my wrist. Surprised, I investigated it. It worked just like it did inside the machine, except I couldn't alter my body. Being in that thing had changed me.

Colin's face appeared on the screen at my wrist. "This is my profile page, dude. You can come here and talk to me whenever you want."

"This is insane, man," I said. "I can't believe I can still see you."

He agreed, laughing. "Have fun trying to pay attention in Math with this on your arm."

"What are you doing in there?" I asked, still confused. "Are you going to save Tommy?"

"I don't know if we can. I don't know if he wants to be saved. But we're gonna try. Maybe we can convince him to turn back." He gave me a somber look and turned his head. Something in the distance caught his eye and he smiled. "Don't worry about me," he said. "I can handle myself."

"Alright."

"Don't tell anyone."

"Sure."

"I'll talk to you tomorrow."

Less than an hour had passed since we entered the arcade. It felt like it had been much longer than that. My mind was spinning. When I reached my house, I could hear my parents arguing from the street. They were screaming at each other. It was over money, again. I stood outside and was suddenly overwhelmed by the desire to go back to the arcade — to go back in the game. To run, to fly, to be free.

But I felt guilty. I'd promised my mom I wouldn't stay out all night. She couldn't sleep when I did. She'd lie awake until dawn if she had too, just to know I was safe. They were still yelling. I wished Colin was there to make me laugh. I slumped my shoulders and climbed the fire escape, sneaking in through my bedroom window to avoid their argument.

Exhausted, I crashed onto my bed. Just as I started to fall asleep my mom knocked and came in. She sat at the foot of my bed, a heavy weight in her eyes. Remembering the module on my wrist, I hid my arm beneath the covers.

"What is it, Grant? What have you got there?" she asked. "Have you been shoplifting again?" She pulled away the covers and grabbed my wrist. She couldn't see it. To her, there was nothing there.

"Mom," I complained, looking at the module in disbelief.

"Sorry," she said, standing and crossing her arms. "I just worry about you, that's all." She walked back to the door. "Thank you for coming home tonight."

"No problem."

"I love you."

"I love you too."

I rolled my eyes when she closed the door, then I passed out. I slept without dreaming; not that any dream could compare with what I just experienced.

Colin pinged me in the middle of the night. I awoke dazed and stared at my wrist.

"Hey man, I just wanted you to know that I might not be coming back," he said.

"What are you talking about," I wiped my eyes.

"I like it here. Your parents might always be screaming, but at least they notice you. I've got nothing out there. I think maybe this place is just meant for me."

"Colin," I started, but he cut me off.

"Grant, listen," he shook his head. "You're my friend, my best friend. If you want to find me, you know where I'll be."

The screen flickered and he was gone. I tried contacting him several times, but he didn't respond. Emotionally drained, I closed my eyes and tried to sleep.

I woke before sunrise, my head throbbing. I felt numb, like nothing mattered. After being inside the game, the real world was lackluster, pointless. The only place I wanted to be was back inside, where I was free.

I tried contacting Colin again on my wrist module. He responded, but he looked different, his image was distorted on the screen.

"What's going on?" I asked. "Are you still in there?"

"Grant," he said, his eyes wandering and unfocused. "I was wrong last night. This place wasn't meant for us. Whatever you do don't come back here. Don't try to save me. I'm sorry. It's too late."

His image sparked in and out with static interference, as his body was engulfed by flames.

"Colin, what are you talking about? What's going on?"

"My name is not Colin. I have become Logi," he growled.

I had no idea what he meant. What was Logi? The name of the device? A part of the game? I tried to make sense of what he was saying. I asked him about the others.

"Tommy and Derek have divinified," he said. "I will be joining them shortly. I won't be coming back."

Tears welled in my eyes. I couldn't lose my only friend, not like this. "I'm coming to get you," I said, jumping out of bed.

"It's too late," he warned. "Don't come. It's not safe. Save yourself..." his voice trailed off and he was gone.

I grabbed my backpack and sprinted out the door. The sun was rising as I scaled the ladder to the roof of the arcade. It would open in a few hours, so I had to act quick. I made my way through the duct work and ran past the rows of games to the back room where the dingy pinball machine sat propped against the wall. I couldn't believe it, I forgot to bring a coin.

I looked around frantically, trying to find another way to the hidden door. It was hopeless. I was ready to give up when I spotted it. There, lying on the dank carpet, as if left for me, was the silver dollar attached to a string.

I picked it up and placed it into the coin slot. It dropped in and I pulled it back out. The machine lit up and the floor spun as the hidden door revealed itself. I tried to reach Colin, but only rough static came through.

As I placed my hand on the glowing sphere, I wondered if I would ever make it back out, or if the allure would be too great for me to overcome. Joy shot through my arm and filled me as green light consumed my body. It was exhilarating. White light flooded my vision.

I took flight with unbridled determination. I was able to locate Colin quickly using my wrist module. He had taken a new form. He was a massive volcano, spewing molten lava, hot rocks exploding deep within his caldera. I shouted his name, but my voice was lost in the chaos of the great volcano's churning. I tried to contact him through the module, but his profile screen showed nothing but fiery lava.

"Colin!" I shouted, as loud as I could.

"My name is Logi," a deep gurgling voice came from the volcano.

I refused to call him that and yelled his name again, "Colin! You have to fight it! Turn back now!"

"Never," the voice rumbled. I watched as a giant spectral arm rose from the central vent of the volcano. It climbed above me, into the sky, and swung down at me. I tried to evade it, but it was too fast. It grabbed me in midair. I struggled against the force, but it wasn't trying to hurt me. I felt no pain. Instead, I was overwhelmed by the sensation of bliss. It was incredible. It was Colin. He was infusing my body with the power he now felt. Not only was there enigmatic joy, but I had complete control over it. I felt internal peace and a oneness with the universe that I had never known. My friend was trying to show me all that I could have here.

Slipping away into feeling, I thought of my mother. That worried look in her eyes. The words she said to me when she left my room last night. None of this was real.

"Colin, stop." I fought against the flooding emotions. "You have to try!"

"It's too late," his voice echoed from the volcano. "There's only one way."

The volcano rumbled; lava sputtered from the vents as cracks formed along its surface.

"I must destroy myself."

"Colin, don't!"

"Self-destruction sequence will begin in five, four, three, two..."

There was a loud explosion and tremors rippled through the massive rock structure. The volcano began to topple, rocks cascaded down towards the smoldering lava. I was tumbling down with it, still caught in the fiery hand.

I tried to protest, to tell him to stop as my eyes rolled back into my head in ecstasy. White light filled my vision, heat radiated beneath my flesh. I reached out my right hand towards Colin, as if I might reach him. Then I placed my left hand on my heart and closed my eyes.

When I opened them, I was back in the small dark room. I looked to the holographic screen on my wrist. On Colin's profile page, black smoke dissipated into the wind. And then there was nothing.

I stared at the green orb. I was angry, angrier than I'd ever been. I took the lighter fluid from my backpack and doused the entire room. I lit a match and tossed it on the floor. Flames leapt at my feet as the carpet burned. I ran. When I made my way out to the roof, the far end of the building was engulfed in flames. I slid down the ladder and ran, but he was already there, the sheriff's dog had sniffed me out. I couldn't outrun him.

. . .

Cuffed at the station, I tried to explain to Sheriff LeBuff and Officer LeBlanc what had happened. I tried to show them my wrist module, and they both took turns examining my arm, but they couldn't see it. I told them about Johnny, Tommy, Derek, and Colin. My story piqued their interest, but I had no way of proving it. I know I did the right thing when I set the arcade on fire, but Sheriff LeBuff said he'd still have to charge me with arson. I told you poor kids like me always get the short end of the stick.

That night I lay awake on the cot in my holding cell. I kept looking at the module on my wrist, hoping Colin would try to reach me. I feared the orb was still out there. If it was, I guessed there was still a chance I'd see Colin again someday. I stared at the module all night, knowing I would have to live with it as a reminder of what I had lost. Maybe for the rest of my life.

In the morning I was surprised when the two men who came to transport me to the juvenile detention center were both dressed in dark suits and sunglasses. I was nervous and unsure of where they were taking me as I sat in the back of their black SUV. When I saw the barred windows and razor wire of Belmont Asylum, I knew.

Colin was a friend of mine. He's gone now. I hope I'm not, too.

22

CAMPBELL'S QUARRY

My friend Chris called and invited me to come over and see his new apartment. He had recently moved out of his parents' house and was excited to have friends visit his new digs.

Chris moved to Kirksland, into the third-floor apartment of an old building right beside the old Campbell's Quarry.

Before ending the call, Chris said, "Wait till you see the place, it's crazy. It's the only three-story building in the whole town. And dude, have I got some weird tales to tell you!"

I'd passed through the small town of Kirksland many times while driving along I-29 on my way to other places. It was sort of in the middle of nowhere, and if you blinked, you'd miss it. The town was basically just an old quarry surrounded by a few crumbling buildings.

A long time ago, maybe a hundred years or more, the quarry was a big deal. The company that owned the quarry had built houses nearby for the workers and their families. There was a company general store that sold everything from clothes to coffee, a small company bank, a United States Post Office, and an old rail line that ran right up to and ended at the quarry. Back then the stone from the quarry was transported by rail, east, towards DC. I'm not sure what kind of stone they were selling, but the owners made a killing. Investors poured in and they say half the houses in Boltsville were built from money from the old quarry.

I'm not sure what exactly happened, but as the years passed the demand for the stone they were mining dwindled and the company had to let most of their workers go. Eventually, the train stopped coming, too. Now-a-days the old tracks are rusted and overgrown with grass, weeds, and wildflowers.

The drive from Boltsville only took twenty minutes. Upon entering Kirksland, I rounded the final corner, crossed over the rusty tracks, and pulled into a gravel parking lot next to the building where Chris lived. The sky was painted with dark red and orange as the sun set. The colors reflected a reddish tint onto the building.

I got out of my car and had a good look at the building. It was old. Really, really old. White plaster peeled from the sides revealing the stone and bricks that held the building up. There wasn't a straight angle on the building. It seemed to be leaning in every direction at once. Decades of dynamite blasts must have shaken and rattled the building at its foundations. I was surprised it was still standing.

I walked around to the front, gravel crunching under my shoes, and climbed four wabbly wooden steps to the entrance. I opened the door and walked into what I figured was the lobby. It was a post office. The Kirksland Post Office. I looked around and called out, but no one answered. The place was old, it even smelled old. Everything looked original, like nothing new had been added in a century. The shelves, counters, and floors were all made of varnished wood. The metal cash register on the counter was in mint condition, it looked like it came right out of an old western. The posters on the wall were yellowed and had curled edges. None of them were in color, they were all sepia tone. One had a photo of Theodore Roosevelt on it.

It was weird.

I pulled my phone out and sent Chris a text. I immediately received the reply: *Entrance around back.*

Gravel crunched as I walked to the back. Once there, I found a rusted metal door at the base of an outcrop that jutted awkwardly from the building. I opened the door to find a long wooden staircase. It ran up all three stories. It was rickety and the stairs were crooked.

Here goes nothing, I thought, and climbed all three stories of the creaky stairs.

I knocked on the door. It was unlocked and swung open, so I entered.

"Yo, Chris!" I shouted.

"Come on in," Chris called. "I'm in the living room."

And that's where I found him. We high fived and Chris offered to show me around.

"How about a tour?" he said. It took less than a minute.

"Dude, this is crazy! The entire building is crooked. It'd be a perfect setting for a horror movie."

Chris laughed, "Yeah right!"

Before returning to the living room we made a pit stop in the kitchen and grabbed a couple of cold beers.

Settling into a large bean bag chair in Chris' living room, I was eager to hear the bizarre stories he mentioned on the phone. Chris lit a joint and passed it to me.

Taking the joint, I mused, "If this old place could talk, imagine the stories..." I took a hit and passed the joint back to Chris.

"I've only been here a week and I think I've already heard the walls talk!" He paused to take a puff. "Check this out," he said, holding in the smoke and passing the joint back to me. "So, I met the girl who lives downstairs, her name's Anna. She's pretty hot, dude. She's got these beautiful green eyes. Anyways, she told me about a guy who had lived in the building decades ago."

Chris said it was a true story and I nodded, although with Chris you never knew if he was telling the truth or pulling your leg.

"The guy lived with his elderly mother and was messed up. He thought stuff was real when it wasn't. I think he hallucinated or something — heard voices."

I couldn't help but say, "You mean like hearing the walls talk?"

Chris laughed at my wisecrack and I handed him the joint again.

"Supposedly the stuff he heard made him go insane. And one

night he climbed to the attic, scratched a note on the wall with a knife, and hung himself."

"Whoa..." was all I could say.

"Yeah man, I actually went to the attic to see for myself, and there it was, writing literally scratched into the wall." Chris looked pretty serious.

"For real?"

"Yeah dude."

"What did it say, could you read it?" I asked.

"Parts of it. The guy was totally out of his mind. Lots of it's gibberish. I think some of it might have even been in Chinese. The guy etched stuff all over the walls. I mean all over, from top to bottom. There are sketches of the towers up on Tower Hill, weird diagrams, and even, like, octopuses," he said, exhaling. "Is that even how you say it? Octopuses?"

We both had a good laugh.

"The guy was seriously twisted. He wrote that the building was haunted by an evil spirit that wanted to steal his soul and make him do bad things. Craziness. The rope he used to kill himself is even still tied to one of the rafters."

I was stunned to silence.

"You wanna go up there and check it out?" Chris offered.

"Not today, dude. That's insane."

"Scared?"

"It's just creepy. I don't need to see some guy's suicide note. Tell me why you wanted to live here again?"

Chris laughed and put out the joint. He leaned back in his chair and swigged his beer. "It gets weirder. Anna, the girl downstairs, told me another story. It's the absolute craziest story ever. A few days ago, when she was getting ready to go to sleep, her cat suddenly started hissing. It's, like, a black cat. At first, she said she thought it was a mouse or something. But then the cat backed into a corner. Aw man, it arched its back and started hissing and clawing at the air."

Chris paused to let the scene sink in.

"And?"

"Anna looked at her cat in the corner, arched back, its hair sticking straight up, hissing.

'It's ok kitty.' she said, trying to calm it down, 'What's gotten into you little buddy?' A long guttural growl gurgled from the cat. Anna was scared. She told her cat, 'It's ok buddy, you're safe, nothing's gonna hurt you.' But her cat wouldn't relax, man. So, she tried again. This time she was like, 'It's okay. You're a good kitty, I love you.' Then from behind her, so close she could feel the breath on her neck, this deep harsh voice said, 'I don't love you!' Anna turned around but nothing was there."

"And she still lives here?" I couldn't help but ask.

"Yeah, she's, like, from around here. Her family's lived in town forever."

I looked at Chris. He was pulling my leg. I was sure of it.

"Yeah right, I bet she's already gone!"

Chris just sat back, laughed, and sipped his beer.

We continued talking about all the weird stuff that had happened there as the beer cans piled up on the table. When I looked at my phone to see what time it was, it was a lot later than I thought.

"Wow, I gotta get going," I said. "I hate to end our conversation, but it's late and I need to be up early tomorrow."

We high fived and did the man hug. Chris walked me to the door. "Here's a final thought," he said. "I wonder if decades of explosions at the quarry roused some ancient spirit, man. Think of all the stories around town. This is where it's all coming from. This building, its alive. It's possessed. It wants our souls. All of our souls."

Chris paused. He tried to keep a straight face but started laughing. "I'm just messing with you!" he said.

"I'm getting the heck out of here. Later."

"Later dude."

Chris closed the door behind me, and I started down the staircase. I was a little buzzed and the way down seemed long, way longer than when I was walking up. How long does it take to walk down three flights of stairs? It felt like I'd already descended ten stories and had ten more to go. I'd look down at my feet as I walked, but when I'd look up, I hadn't moved at all. I had no idea what was going on. It was so bizarre. I wasn't making any progress, so I started going faster. I was bounding down the steps two at a time when I felt someone, or something, breathing down my neck. I panicked and started running, faster and faster. Sweat broke out, I could feel it on my forehead, and I kept running, faster, and faster still.

When I finally reached the landing, I was covered in sweat. I opened the door and ran out into the night. I stopped to catch my breath. There was a new moon in the sky and layers of clouds blocked the stars. It was so dark. Too dark.

I ran to my car, gravel crunching underfoot. I jumped in, shut and locked the door. I jammed the key in the ignition and twisted the key to start the car. I shifted into reverse and pressed my foot on the gas pedal. Wheels spun, kicking up gravel as I backed out of the parking space and dropped the car into drive. I was about to turn right out of the parking lot when my phone rang.

I stopped the car to answer the call, "Hello."

"Yo dude, when you coming over? It's been like hours since we talked."

It was Chris. This had to be a joke.

"Good one Chris."

"What?"

"What, what?"

"Seriously, where are you?"

"What are you talking about, I just left your place."

Chris laughed and I got nervous.

"No really. I just left," I said, seriously.

"What are you talking about?"

"I just left your place in Kirksland."

"Kirksland?"

"Yeah."

"Dude, no one's lived in Kirksland for, forever!"

I looked in the rearview mirror and slowly lowered my phone. I could hear Chris, he was still talking, but I wasn't listening to him. I looked but couldn't believe what I saw. I closed and rubbed my eyes, but when I opened them, I saw the same thing. What. Was. Going. On.

The building — or what was left of it — was in ruins. Sections of the walls stood, but the roof, windows, and the rest of it had collapsed, along with the staircase — a long time ago. It was a pile of rubble. Vines and weeds covered the fallen structure.

I'd been inside for hours, hanging with Chris, or so I thought. What was I doing for the last three hours?! Who had called to invite me? Who answered my texts?

I decided not to stay a second longer. I took my foot off the brake and floored it, peeling out onto the road. I sped towards the old tracks. That's when the railroad crossing lights started flashing and clanging. I jammed on the brakes, skidding to a stop. Then I heard an old train whistle blowing.

"Come on man, there's no train, just go!" I shouted. Whatever was going on, I wasn't waiting to find out. I floored it, crossing over the tracks as I high-tailed it out of Kirksland and away from the old quarry. I vowed to never go back.

A few miles down the road, police lights flashed behind me. I was scared to death and didn't want to stop, but when the police car pulled alongside me, and I saw Officer LeBlanc barking at me to pull over, that's what I did.

My heart was racing as he approached the driver's side window. I didn't know what to do. What if he smelled the alcohol? He knocked on my window with his flashlight and I rolled it down.

"Officer, you won't believe what just happened!"

He never asked if I'd been drinking. He didn't mention my speeding at all. Police deputy LeBlanc just leaned in my window, looked at me with his silver eyes, and said, "Tell me everything."

23

A PAPER UNICORN

Paper. That's all the thing was. A heaping pile of paper. Two stories stacked from floor to ceiling. A real fire trap if you ask me. I'd settled many estates for Chatham County and the city of Savannah during my long career, but this one proved to be the most peculiar.

The deceased owner passed some weeks prior. In his sleep, if you must know. No family, no will, no one claiming him as their own. It was my job to locate his financials, identify any heirs or kin, and settle his affairs as quickly as possible.

Upon entering the house on Barnard Street, the first thing that hit me was the smell. My god, I gagged. Apparently, the man in question had kept a large supply of raw squid in his refrigerator. Not to eat, but to dissect and study. An odd detail, but not as odd as the sketches and painstaking notes I found regarding this effort. The functions of the nervous system of the species seemed to be of particular interest to this man.

After his death, the electrical company cut his power and the creatures had decomposed into a putrefied black slime that oozed from the refrigerator, coating the kitchen floor with rancid oil.

Once past the putrid smell, I took a closer look. It appeared the man had been a great collector, of all things. Really! The intricate notebooks he kept gave me the feeling that he was looking for something. God knows what.

The man who had resided in the home must have been a complete shut-in. He'd put great effort into his clutter. I was forced to rummage through it all, isles of notebooks and journals, hoping to find his records and financial documentation.

Shelves were built into every wall, floor to ceiling. All of them crammed with books, notebooks, photographs, and trinkets. Whether a hoarder or avid reader, the books he kept were of a notable kind.

Large volumes of philosophy: Aristophanes, Aristotle, Aurelius and Aquinas, Cicero, Descartes, Kant, Locke, Hegel, Hobbes, and Hume. Plato. Smith and Spinoza. Wittgenstein! But not just western minds, Buddhist texts, the Tao Te Ching, the Bhagavad Gita, the Upanishads, and more. There were books about Japanese water gardens, Eastern architecture, Chinese calligraphy, the art of Hokusai.

He collected many books of art from the New York contemporaries like Basquiat. Photographers, Absurdists, Cubists, Impressionists, Sculptors, Goya and Velasquez. The Renaissance greats, DaVinci and Michelangelo, to the religious works that predated them. He even had books on the sarcophagi and hieroglyphs of Ancient Egypt. Sheet music from Bach to Wagner, and a collection of wax spools with god knows what recorded on them.

At first glance the interior of the building appeared to be in complete disarray, drowned in an endless sea of paper — the complete recorded history of man. After a closer look I realized it was all quite organized. There was a section dedicated to psychology with the complete works of Freud and William James, literary works from the Odyssey to the Great Gatsby, a section dedicated to engineering with detailed and numbered blueprints of everything from buildings to factories, airplanes to missiles, turbines, hydroelectrical dams, nuclear powerplants, and a full section dedicated to the excavation of quarries and mines.

Textbooks on everything from botany to neuroscience, geology to quantum mechanics. Language books and books in different languages, from European origins to Arabic, Cantonese, Hebrew, Hindi, Macedonian, Mandarin, Punjabi, Quechua, and Yiddish.

But, for every printed page the man owned he had two more penned by his own hand. Hand drawn sketches of every kind of flora and fauna, all notated in Latin. He'd written his own philosophical treatises, codes of law, a book of world history. Diagram after diagram, model after model. I'd never seen so many math equations in one place in my entire life. It was incredible. Really, it was.

I stood in the man's living room in complete awe. Above his mantle hung an intricately drafted model of nine towers built into a stone hill. The structures, varying in height and arranged in an odd spiral, were drawn from multiple points of view, each to scale.

After wandering around the place for several hours, I finally found the man's study. A hand drawn topographical map was spread across his desk. There were several clearly marked locations on it. What they were or where they were, I don't know.

On top of the map sat a journal of red leather. Embossed on the cover the words, *Book 3 of 3*. Curious, I opened it. It appeared to be some kind of genealogical study, penned by the deceased's own hand. It started with the words, *After losing his brother in the Civil War my grandfather, Coniferous Campbell, headed south.*

According to the journal, the fella's grandfather was a carpet bagger, but it didn't say from where. He made his way to North Carolina and married a southern belle, Marianne LeClair, of Sampson County. Apparently that girl was a freethinking intellectual and heiress to a railroading industrialist's fortune. The two used her dowry to buy up swaths of land from Northern Georgia, all the way down to the Florida pan handle. The end of slavery had changed a lot of things in America. Especially in the South. Farmers who were already in debt were crushed by labor cost and the land was cheap and ripe to be plucked.

The two had planned to build up local communities throughout the recently freed states by funding new business and managing the sales and distribution of land. But Marianne, against her nature, died giving birth to their first and only child, a son named Oliver.

The journal claimed that Coniferous was so distraught over the death of his wife that he paid little mind to his young child. Instead, he focused his energies fulfilling the ideals of his dearly departed Marianne. He worked tirelessly to build something greater than himself.

Coniferous became the pride of many counties. He harvested turpentine from the extensive pineland under his dominion, built and managed his own chain of marine stores along the coast, and used every penny of profit to build churches and community buildings. He was the lead financier of everything in antebellum Georgia.

Oliver appeared to have been an afterthought. As an only child, a very wealthy afterthought.

According to the journal, Oliver was a bitter disappointment to his father. A drunken buffoon, he cavorted with the lowest of the low in the brothels and barrooms of Savannah. By the time of his father's death, Oliver had nine children from six women, most of them born out of wedlock.

Through his drunken debauchery and careless spending, he squandered all of what remained of the family fortune, trading the last plot of priceless pineland for a single case of whiskey. During Oliver's sixty-third year, his final wife, Annice Clark, a seamstress and whore, gave birth to his thirteenth child, a son named Jasper.

Jasper was the owner of the home on Barnard Street, and the author of the journal. He'd grown up in the squalor of his father's broken dreams. At Oliver's side in barrooms and you know where else. Hardly the proper life for a child. Despite this, Jasper excelled academically. The journal charted his many merit badges, awards, and aptitude scores. At the age of eighteen, World War II was in full swing. Instead of going to college, Jasper joined the navy and spent the next several years of his life in the Pacific, fighting against the Japanese. He was a heavily decorated officer for his efforts during the war.

When the war was over, Jasper continued his military role in

Europe, helping to commission and maintain the nuclear installations for allied countries. After his father's death he requested and was granted an honorable discharge. He returned to Savannah to settle his father's affairs. The journal ended there. There was no mention of his many siblings, or what the young man did with his life upon returning home. I assumed the next sixty years of his life had been spent right at the very desk I was sitting.

In the drawers of the desk were his financial records. I'd already wasted too much time lost in the peculiarities of man's home to look them all over. I skimmed a few of the document, before leaving. He'd been receiving a pension from the U.S. government since his discharge. It was a modest sum, and I wondered if that was all he'd been living on for all these years.

Aside from that, the only thing of interest was a long beer tally and a series of letters and meeting notes from the local American Legion, Post 135. After dinner, my curiosity got the best of me and I went down to the legion hall to inquire about the man.

I asked the bartender if she knew Jasper Campbell, and she raised her eyebrows and shook her head no. No one at the bar had ever heard of him. Not wanting to give up that easy, I pressed on. Finally, one of the patrons asked me, "Are you talking about Dom Wilkins? Lived over on Barnard, passed away just a couple of weeks ago?"

I had no idea who he was talking about, but both the address and time of death sounded right. I furrowed my brow in thought. Suddenly, I remembered seeing the name Dom Wilkins on some of the stationary in the man's house.

"Yes, that's right. I must have gotten his name mixed up," I lied.

Next thing I knew, we were all raising our glasses and toasting this Dom Wilkins. Jasper Campbell must have spent much of his life living under that alias. They all knew Dom. He'd been coming to the Post every night for the past fifty years.

I had trouble believing it at first, that this apparent genius I'd spent the day admiring had been belly up to a bar every night of his life.

Just mentioning his name brought tears to one of the men's eyes.

"We sure miss him," another said, and they all nodded in agreement.

Apparently, he'd been a beloved patron. He'd come in around dinner each night and sit at the end of the bar doing crossword puzzles. He'd have a few beers, tell a few jokes, eat, and go home. Aside from his sharp wit and clever tongue, none of them seemed to know much about his personal life. When I asked if they knew anything about his family, they all just shook their heads no.

They said he never spoke about the war, or his time in the military. Still he saluted and patted the back of every service man or woman who walked through the door. Aside from chatting it up at the bar, they said Dom's only other apparent interest were the stars. Every clear night he'd set up his telescope in Forsythe park. They said he would talk about the constellations like he'd written their names in the sky with his own fingers, and that when there was a meteor shower, he'd claim to know the chemical makeup of each shooting star by the color of its tail.

With a steady buzz and a few good stories, I finally made my way home. That night I lay awake in my bed thinking about this strange and clandestine man. I wonder what it was he was looking for? What it was he was hiding from? It struck me funny that no one had come to claim his body, his personal effects, or possessions. I'm sure that some of the folks from the neighborhood might have dropped by and plucked a thing or two, but what about his family? The youngest of thirteen and no one came to claim him as their own?

Upon reaching my office in the morning I was shocked to find that his estate had been settled in the night. It was unprecedented. I asked for more details but there were none to be had. At the first opportunity, I excused myself and ran over to the house on Barnard Street. Much to my surprise the street was blocked off by police at both ends. I couldn't see clearly over the blockade, but an unmarked moving truck was parked in front of the house. Men in black suits were unloading box after box of his possessions, all of his books, all of his notes, into the truck. By the afternoon the house was empty, and every shred of the man's life work gone.

24

THE SPRING HOUSE

Far below the parapets of Tower Hill and deep beneath the manicured lawns of Sycamore Street, water trickles slowly through the soil, carving a path down through black rocks that fortify the water table of Rustle County. This ever-churning, deep well that feeds the Black Water River can be heard calling out to the children of Boltsville in a hushed whisper, "Come to the Spring House."

The Spring House is not much to look at, a stout stone building with mossy shingles and vines climbing its crumbling white plaster walls. It was originally built by Abraham Campbell as a place to preserve food and store root vegetables during the winter. He fled to America to escape religious persecution. He thought the quiet countryside of Rustle County would be a safe place for his family to start anew. He was wrong.

But that was long ago, and the tragedies that befell his family are all but forgotten. The Spring House and much of the old Campbell estate still stand. Expertly engineered in their time, the buildings are now dilapidated, overgrown with tall grasses, the paint peeling, the ornate wooden trim rotten and bare.

Sometimes children wander onto the property, not knowing exactly why they are there. They pass the old stables and servant quarters. They follow the gravel driveway, past the broken windows of the greenhouses and past the overgrown fields, until they reach the Spring House, sitting at the bottom of a slope off of the main house.

But children are not the only ones who come here. Others may find themselves wandering the vast estate too, looking for something lost long ago.

Deputy LeBlanc strode through the tall wet grass, flashlight in hand. It was near dawn and the birds chirped sweetly from the brush. Approaching the Spring House, he found three bicycles lying in the dewy grass. A plastic toy flashlight lay on the ground next them, its bulb still burning dully.

LeBlanc sniffed at the air and approached the peeling wooden door. He pushed it open and entered the building. The ceilings were low, and he had to hunch to stand in the dark, damp room. The sound of rushing water echoed across the exposed stone walls.

The building had an old dirt floor, covered with dusty rocks and rotting wood. A short ladder lead to a small loft. LeBlanc didn't need to climb it to see what was up there, dirty wooden planks and cobwebs.

In the far corner a piece of plywood sat on the floor. Officer LeBlanc pulled it away, exposing a crude stairwell of stone. He looked down to the bottom of the stairs at wet rocks and running water. He crouched down and climbed inside.

The water was shallow, barley up to his ankles. He sloshed into the tight quarters, shining his flashlight. The space was enclosed. The water came in from the floor at one end and ran towards the far wall. He crawled to the far wall. Kneeling, he felt around beneath the surface of the water. Allowing his hand to follow the current, he found a small opening in the rocks. He leaned forward and reached through it. Water cascaded around and below his searching hand. The hole was deep and narrow, its walls slimy and wet.

The bikes outside suggested the children who entered the building were far too big to pass through the narrow slit in the stone. A cat could have barley passed through the opening.

Officer LeBlanc shook off his wet arm. He climbed back up the stone stairs, his shoes filled with water and squishing. He looked around the Spring House one last time. There was nothing in there but dusty old rocks and flowing water.

Deputy LeBlanc shut and latched the door behind him. He stood with his hands on his hips, staring at the three bikes lying in the grass. He looked up towards the main house and noticed a light on in one of the upstairs rooms. Officer LeBlanc narrowed his eyes as a figure passed by the window. It stopped. A silhouette stood clearly in the window. It raised its hand and waved.

25

BETTER LEFT ALONE: PART 7

A black cat sat licking its paws on the front porch of the main house as Deputy LeBlanc climbed the wobbled steps. The front door was etched with scrollwork and centered with a stained glass window. He could hear music lightly playing inside.

He raised his hand to knock and the door creaked open. A white-haired woman in a long paisley dress stood before him. The age lines on her face deepened as she smiled. Her green eyes sparkled like a cat's.

"Hell-woe, Craven," she said, motioning for him to come inside. "I've been expecting you."

Dumbfounded, LeBlanc ducked through the front door.

"I'm sorry," he asked. "Do I know you?"

"Yes, of course. Anna Kirksguard. We've met many times before."

Deputy LeBlanc remembered everyone he'd ever met in town, but he could not place her. He scratched his temple and looked around. The plaster walls were cracked with the laths exposed in places, but the intricate woodwork was well preserved. A staircase led to the second floor, the banisters, spindles, and newels stained in a dark rich color. A hallway leading to the kitchen passed beneath an above catwalk. To his right was a single paneled door and to his left a closed pair of heavy pocket doors.

"You're looking well," Anna said, sliding open the pocket doors to reveal a small sitting room. "Won't you sit down?"

LeBlanc entered the sitting room. A loveseat and two armchairs surrounded a low coffee table. A record spun on the phonograph in the corner of the room. Soft jazz. LeBlanc turned to look at the woman, this Anna. She smiled at him kindly.

"How do I know you again?" he asked.

"Don't you worry about that now. Why don't you have a seat while I go get us some refreshments?" Anna said, exiting to the kitchen.

Still confused, LeBlanc sat down onto the loveseat, trying to shake free the cobwebs. He looked across the foyer at the light coming from beneath the far door. He listened. He could hear the buzz of the light-bulb in the stairwell, the faint tumbling of a washing machine.

Anna returned with a silver tray and placed it down on the coffee table. She poured two steaming cups of tea, placed one on a saucer with a madeleine cookie, and handed it to Deputy LeBlanc. LeBlanc sniffed the cup and examined the cookie with his fingers before putting the saucer down on the coffee table.

"Not hungry?" Anna asked, sitting.

"What can you tell me about the bicycles I found in your yard?"

"Nothing. I didn't even know they were there until I saw you standing next to them. Is there something you want to tell me?"

"How do you know my name?"

Anna sat upright, gathering herself. She was about to say something when there was a knock on the door.

"I wasn't expecting so many visitors this morning," she said, standing.

Officer LeBlanc watched as the woman made her way to and opened the front door.

"Good morning," she said.

"Anna," Sheriff LeBuff nodded. "More people gone missing at your front door?"

Anna disregarded the sheriff's question and stuck her nose into the air. Officer LeBlanc watched in disbelief as his senior officer entered the sitting room.

"LeBlanc," the sheriff said, helping himself to a handful of the cookies from the tray and sitting down.

"Craven's looking well."

"How much have you told him already?" LeBuff snarled.

Anna took her seat, opposite the sheriff. "We were just getting started," she said, turning to deputy LeBlanc. "Please forgive Gerald's temperament. He hasn't liked me since his sister Monica went missing."

"You and that loser Teddy Bridges were the only witnesses. She disappeared right in front of your eyes."

Deputy LeBlanc's eyes pinballed from side to side as the two spoke. "What are you talking about?" he asked. "When did that happen?"

"It was the summer after I graduated from college," Anna said.

"It was forty years ago," LeBuff added, lowering his head. "The case is still unsolved. Along with hundreds of others. The initial investigation went nowhere. That's why I joined the academy. I never really wanted to be a cop."

"Gerald was a gifted baseball player."

"How do you remember that?" the sheriff laughed. He and Anna looked at each other and smiled. "Alright," he said. "You might as well start from the beginning. When was the first time you remember hearing about someone going missing in Rustle County?"

Anna took a sip of her tea and sat back in her chair. "It wasn't until I was thirteen. Our family sheltered my brother and I, so we never heard any of the gossip in town. My cousin told me the story when she got back from summer camp at Camp Manasquam. I can still remember the terrified look in her eyes."

"Camp Manasquam?" LeBlanc asked.

"Yeah," Sheriff LeBuff answered. "It's just north of Tower Hill, on the other side of the river. Been abandoned since the eighties."

"Where is your cousin now?" LeBlanc turned to Anna.

"Dead. Like all those who have carried our family name."

26

ENDLESS SUMMERS

E llie stood in the rain, eagerly awaiting her lodge assignment. A lean and athletic twelve-year-old, she relished the opportunity to prove she was just as strong, just as fast, and even smarter than the boys her age. Though she just arrived, she could already tell she made the right decision when she talked her mother into letting her come to Camp Manasquam for the summer. At any other camp the rain would have driven all activities indoors and she'd be huddled around a table doing watercolors or some other boring craft. Not here at Manasquam.

She watched intently as the counselors, even Mr. Scanlon the camp director, walked nonchalantly among the campers. They spoke clearly as they instructed and organized their groups, before marching off towards their lodges.

That night, at the campfire, Mr. Scanlon presented the Manasquam creed: *Meet Life on Life's Terms*. "The world you'll live in over the next seventy or eighty years will not be all sunny days. The challenges you'll face will likely be unfair, sometimes shattering. Over the summer you will learn to triumph over difficulties through courage and discipline. The lessons learned will serve you for the rest of your lives." He looked up around the campfire. "Now go to your lodges and get some rest. Calisthenics at 0600. Move!"

Ellie met Alfred the following Wednesday, the first day it didn't rain. She'd noticed him at the swimming challenges. He moved through the water like an eel, leaving barely a ripple behind him. For all her speed and technique, Alfred beat her to the fifty-yard buoy effortlessly.

He walked over to her, rubbing his long hair with a towel. "You're pretty fast." He smiled.

Sitting in the shade, Ellie answered. "At least you didn't say 'for a girl'." She tried to suppress the little tingle his smile had triggered.

"Why would I have said that?"

Ellie looked up at the boy. "Well, I am, you know. A girl."

"So what? You're a damn fast swimmer. I don't think anyone can keep up with you." He grinned. "Except me, of course."

"Oh really?" She slapped the boy on the shoulder. "You just wait."

Alfred made an exaggerated grimace and held his shoulder. "For that you have to join me and the rest of the club at lunch."

"Club?"

"Yeah." He lifted his chin. "We run this place."

In the mess hall during lunch, Ellie joined Alfred, at a mixed table of girls and boys.

"...if we don't catch up with the Russians in space, we're all going to be Communists," one of the boys was saying.

"They're so horrible," a girl with pigtails exclaimed. "They sent that poor dog, Laika, up into space and left it to die." There were several nods around the table.

Alfred sat, placing his tray on the table. He gave Ellie a small smile and turned to the girl in pigtails, "Bella, everything dies. It's logical to sacrifice a dog to find out what might happen to people when they go up." He looked around the group before starting on his grilled cheese sandwich. "She probably didn't last very long."

Bella hung her head. "Poor little thing, all alone."

"We'll beat them. They're just ahead 'cause they grabbed up all the Nazi rocket scientists." The speaker was the tall, soft-looking boy

Ellie had seen forcing a younger kid to give up his rain parka during check-in. She wasn't happy to see he was a part of the group.

Alfred noticed her disapproving look. "Have you met Tyler?" he asked. For his part, Tyler sat up straight and sneered at Ellie.

"No. But I did notice his behavior at check-in," Ellie said.

Alfred raised his eyebrows and turned to the pudgy boy. "Tyler, this is Ellie, a new friend of mine."

Tyler's poisonous look melted. "Oh. Nice to meet you," he said, timidly.

The table conversation continued as the campers ate their lunches. When the gong sounded for cleanup, Alfred leaned in, "Everyone's ready for the operation tonight, right?" Ellie gave him an inquisitive look and Alfred smiled. "I'll explain later," he said.

The operation turned out to be chaining the doors shut to the main lodge and the counselors' cabins. The Counselors-in-Training, or CITs, were often the butt of Alfred's pranks. The highlight of the operation was when Mr. Scanlon climbed out of an upstairs window of the main lodge in his boxer shorts. He lost his footing and rolled down the veranda roof, landing in a heap as the entire camp roared with laughter.

Medieval punishments were threatened but no one came forward to name the perpetrators. In a few days camp life returned to normal and the *Great Lockup* disappeared from the campers' conversations. Then the *Photo Operation* shattered the tranquility of Manasquam.

One of Alfred's gang members had noticed that two of the CITs, Brenda and Bobby, were sneaking off to make out in the woods at night. When Alfred learned of it, he produced a camera with a tele-photo lens and sent Davy, the snitch who'd first seen the couple in the woods, to get pictures.

"I got 'em," Davy gasped, handing the camera to Alfred. "They were hugging and kissing and everything."

Alfred slapped Davy on the back. "Good work. Hurry back to your activity so you don't get caught."

"Alfred, why would you?" Ellie frowned.

"This is going to be great." The boy clapped his hands. "I wish I'd have thought of pictures before."

"What are you going to do with them?"

"We're going to have some fun showing just how silly all these strutting idiots really are. Trust me, it'll be a laugh."

Ellie smothered her doubts in the face of Alfred's confidence — he knew so much. Always clever and cunning, he easily manipulated every member of the camp staff. Through his conniving, he'd gained the freedom to secretly move around at will. It was even rumored that he'd sneak into town mounted on his Honda 90 motorbike to buy cigarettes and candy for resale to the campers. He was the leader of the pack, the head of the club, and to Ellie he was becoming something more.

He smiled at her and she found herself drifting into his dark eyes. "Come help me." Her arm tingled where he touched her. "It will be fun. I promise."

Why not? She asked herself.

Ellie whooped for joy with her arms wrapped around Alfred's waist as they zoomed up an old logging road on his motorbike. She held on tightly, grinning from ear to ear as they passed beneath the deep shade of trees and into the sun.

Emerging from the woods, Alfred pulled into the dooryard of an old farmhouse. Ellie shielded her eyes to see the oddly arranged projections atop the ridge of Tower Hill. She looked back to the farmhouse.

"What is this place?" Ellie asked, dismounting.

"You'll see," Alfred said, killing the engine and producing a key. "You're going to get a kick out of this."

Alfred unlocked the door and Ellie followed him into the living room of the farmhouse. It was stacked with unopened boxes of candy, cigarettes, comic books, and other contraband. As she followed Alfred down the hall, Ellie passed the open door of a bedroom filled with piles of cameras, radios, record players, and racks of records.

Before she could ask any questions, Alfred ceremoniously swung open the door to the room at the end of the hall. "This is my office."

He waved her in. A kitchen table was set against the wall holding neat stacks of paper, a pencil cup, and a telephone. An electric typewriter sat on a separate table to the left of the desk and on a third table there was a mimeograph machine and several boxes of stencils.

Alfred grinned self-consciously. "I had to teach myself to type to use all this stuff." With a light touch on her arm, he turned Ellie to face a black velvet curtain in the rear corner of the room. "This is what I wanted to show you."

He pulled enough of the curtain aside for them both to enter. When he dropped the curtain back into place, they were surrounded in total darkness. Despite her brave reputation, Ellie trembled.

"Just enjoy the darkness for a moment," Alfred said, in a comforting voice. Ellie's heart rate and breathing slowed to normal. "Isn't it peaceful? I love the dark, it allows my thoughts to fly. We could be anywhere or anyone." He paused, his breathing a gentle sound beside Ellie.

"But there's more to see." A dim light flicked on to reveal a fully-equipped darkroom.

Alfred stepped away from Ellie. The light went out and was replaced with an eerie red one. Every object in the room appeared to be either a dense black or red in color, including Alfred. He stood near the wall draped in black except for his face.

"Stop. Turn the light back on." Ellie's heart was racing again.

Alfred's calm, compelling voice reassured her. "Photographic paper and film don't react to red light. It's the only way we can see what we're doing. Come here. I'll show you."

In less than an hour, two dozen enlargements of Brenda and Bobby locked together in a sizzling kiss were in the hands of club members for distribution. The scandal erupted the next morning. Rumors flew and gossip burned on the grapevine. Mr. Scanlon was forced to call an emergency assembly. He began by warning the campers of a swift and unerring punishment for violating the Manasquam Code of Conduct.

"This incident, regrettable though it may be, is a clear demonstration of the care and vigilance we exercise at Manasquam. I see no reason why this should come to the attention of any of your parents." He scanned the faces of the children for a moment. "All today's afternoon activities are cancelled. Counselors and CITs, report to my conference room in fifteen minutes."

Alfred sought out Ellie as soon as the staff was closeted with Mr. Scanlon. "The whole club is meeting at the house. Do you remember how to get there?"

Ellie thought for a moment. As she remembered, the road went straight to the farmhouse with no turns or crossing. "Yeah, I guess but..."

The boy took her by the shoulders. "No questions right now. I've got to go into town. Bella is gathering the club so you can go over with her if you're scared." She had been a little scared, but her fear evaporated when he touched her. "I'll meet you there shortly. Do this for me."

Ellie watched the aimless wandering of the campers with contempt. Without adult leadership they were lost.

"I am not like them," she said with a smile, before slipping behind the activity huts and making her way to the old logging road.

When Ellie reached the farmhouse, she found most of the club inside packing cigarettes and candy into their backpacks.

"Who needs Payday bars?" Bella called, holding up a box of candy bars.

Tyler Schmidt, standing beside her, hollered, "How about Milky Ways or Snickers?"

The boy who had taken the photos, Davy, warned the group. "We'll know if any of you eat your stock. If you do, Alfred won't be happy." The last sentence chilled the air, causing all banter and horseplay to stop. "Everyone understand the prices? If you have any trouble, tell me, or Tyler, or Bella." He looked around the room. "Okay, nobody's got anything to do this afternoon, so we should be able to move a lot of snacks. If you need comic books, see Bella on the way out."

The little merchants dispersed, soon followed by Tyler and Davy. Ellie and Bella were left to repack and straighten up the boxes.

"Bella, what's the story here? Whose house is this?"

"It belongs to Alfred." The older girl grunted as she lifted one of the boxes onto the stack. "He told me that it's been in his family for more than fifty years."

"Do his parents know what he's doing here?"

"His parents died." Her voice slowed and softened. "They died a long time ago." She shook her head. "Isn't it just like the boys to leave us to clean up?" She lifted another box.

Ellie pushed a sweat-stuck strand of hair from her forehead. "I'm looking forward to getting in the lake when we get back. Aren't you?"

Bella hesitated. "I don't go in the lake anymore."

"You don't? How come?"

Instead of answering the older girl said, "Why don't we go to Alfred's pond and cool off?"

"Alfred's pond?"

"Yeah. He dammed up a stream at the back of the property to make a pond. I'd take a dip there."

"But, if you won't swim in the lake, why..."

"C'mon. It's only a little ways through the woods."

The pond was really just a swimming hole, only a few strokes across, but it was deep and the water cold and clear.

"I, uh, don't have a suit," Ellie said, a little embarrassed.

"Don't be silly, we're both girls and there's no one else around." Bella stripped off the baggy sweatshirt and the shorts she was wearing and jumped in.

Ellie slipped off her shorts but hesitated to take off her tee shirt.

"Ellie, don't be a chicken. Strip down." Bella ducked under for a moment and came up with a white ball of cloth in her hands. She heaved it toward her clothes on the bank. "Ah, it feels so good to get out of those." When she rolled onto her back it was clear that the white ball was her underwear.

Ellie hated to be dared or to be called chicken. She was out of her shirt and underwear and into the pool in a flash. "Ooo, it's cold," she exclaimed.

"But it feels good, doesn't it?"

After splashing around for a few minutes, Ellie drifted over to Bella. "What's with the candy and stuff?"

Bella smiled. "It's a service we provide to the campers. We sell that crap to the campers cheaper than the camp store and no one gives them a hard time if they want to eat a dozen candy bars or smoke a cigarette."

Ellie's mouth hung open. "But, but, that's not allowed."

Bella laughed. "Your lips are turning blue," she said.

As they stood by the pond drying themselves off with their clothes, Ellie was surprised by the fullness of Bella's breasts, how her hips widened beneath her narrow waist.

Bella caught Ellie's look. "Yeah, I know. You can't tell Alfred, though. You just can't." Bella reached toward Ellie. "Please. I've stayed out of a bathing suit, wrapped myself up like a mummy, and have been wearing my brother's baggy clothes so it won't show."

"But why? I hope I have a shape like yours when I'm older."

"There's no getting older. Alfred won't allow grown-ups in the club. When we start to develop, uhm... Alfred retires us." Bella shuddered. "I don't want to be retired."

"You want to keep doing this stuff?"

"I don't really like it now," the older girl admitted.

"Then why?"

"Haven't you noticed? When Alfred tells you to do something — even something bad — you can't resist. You just do it." Bella sat down on a flat rock and hugged her knees. "When we're not here, some of us stay with Alfred in Boston. We sneak into people's houses while they're sleeping to steal stuff. If I think about it, I'm terrified. But it's a real thrill, too. Alfred makes my fear go away — but it always comes back."

Bella lowered her forehead to her knees. "I guess I'm afraid something bad will happen again, like with the horses," she mumbled.

"Horses?" Ellie's heart rate jumped. "Did you do something to hurt horses?" Ellie loved horses.

"No, we didn't hurt horses. We freed them." Bella rolled over onto her stomach and turned her head away from Ellie. "Let's just enjoy this moment," she said. "Nothing lasts forever."

"No, you have to tell me about the horses."

Bella rested her head on her arms and turned to face Ellie. "When the street cars were electrified, the horses were going to be killed. We broke into the stables and let them all out." She continued softly, "But they stampeded and trampled a young couple and their little baby..." Her eyes filled with tears. "And they killed the horses anyway."

Ellie rested her hand on Bella's shoulder. "You didn't mean to hurt anyone."

"But we did. It's bothered me for all these years."

"Wait. Years? Horse-drawn street cars? What are you talking about? When did that happen?"

Bella rolled onto her back and sat up, "It was 1920. About a year after Alfred found me."

"1920? Bella, that's impossible. What are you talking about?"

"You don't get it yet, do you?" Bella looked at Ellie pityingly. "When do you think I was born?"

"You're playing games," Ellie frowned, but Bella just shook her head. "Okay, have it your way," Ellie continued. "I'm twelve and was born in 1946. You're a couple of years older than me so...1944 or '45?"

"I was born in the Year of Our Lord 1907. I was thirteen when Alfred found me."

"That's ridiculous, you'd be..."

"Fifty years old," Bella cut her off. "Haven't you noticed the breadth of Alfred's knowledge? His ability to wipe away your conscience? To make you feel the exhilaration of total freedom?"

Blushing, Ellie said, "I thought it was uhm...romantic feelings?"

Bella laughed. "Oh, Ellie, Alfred doesn't have those feelings. He will never be older than he was when his family died — he'll be eleven forever."

"Eleven?"

"Forever," Bella confirmed. "And, he passes his gift on to those of us he's chosen." The older girl studied the flow of the water into the swimming hole for a moment. "With one small difference. Alfred's gift only *slows* our aging. Physically, I've aged about a year and a half since 1920. I'm growing up and there's nothing I can do about it."

"But how?" Ellie said, throwing her hands into the air and standing.

"I don't know."

Ellie started to pace. "So, one year for you is like, what, twenty years for you?"

"It seems to vary between twenty and thirty years, yes."

"So, you're going to live to be fourteen hundred years old?"

"I don't know," Bella said, again. "As we begin to grow up, we're retired. For me, it should have been a while ago. I don't know how much longer I'll be able to hide it from him."

"Why bother? Seems like you'd be happy to move on. Aren't you excited to be an adult?"

Bella sighed. "You still don't get it. There's a price for this gift. My friend, Terry, was already a member of the club when I joined." Tears streamed down Bella's face. "Alfred retired him just before we came to camp for the summer," she sobbed, hugging her knees and rocking back and forth.

Ellie sat down and put her arms around Bella. The older girl calmed a little, nestling into Ellie's chest, gulping and hiccupping. "I'm sorry. Terry was so good and now...now..."

"Now what?"

"He's dead. When Alfred blessed him, he told Terry there was only one way to avoid the pain ahead, so Terry killed himself!" Bella wailed, crushing herself against Ellie. "I don't want...don't want..."

"Let's get dressed and get back to camp. Maybe a shower and some rest will make you feel better."

"I can't shower! Someone will see what's happening to me."

"Or maybe you should just go home and tell your parents."

"Go home? I ran away thirty years ago. My parents are probably dead!"

"Well, we're not going to solve the problem sitting here crying."

Ellie stood up, her brain working furiously. "Finish getting dressed and let's head back. I'll think of something. I promise."

After seeing Bella to her bunk, Ellie wandered the camp. She couldn't think of what to do beyond avoiding Alfred and the club. She headed back to her lodge, hoping that a nap would bring a solution to Bella's situation. As she lay in her bunk, all Ellie could see when she closed her eyes was Alfred's face staring back at her. She couldn't escape the feeling that she might be falling into the same trap as Bella.

When Ellie met with Alfred later, instead of ending their friendship as she planned, she was somehow drawn into another one of his late-night escapades. She rode shotgun as Alfred drove his old farm truck to a vending machine warehouse in town. Together they broke in and left with enough cigarettes and candy to restock the farmhouse. Instead of being terrified, the theft and the audacity of their crime thrilled her.

On the way back the two kids regaled each other with different parts of their exploit, laughing at how easy it had been to rip off the warehouse. They made bets on how long, or if, the owners would notice.

"I feel so...so...alive," Ellie crowed.

"Fun, huh?"

After securing the truck, the pair walked back to camp. Heat lighting flashed above Tower Hill.

Ellie looked toward the tower silhouetted in the flashing light. "That's how I feel, full of electricity." She twirled around. "I want to do something else crazy."

Alfred smiled. "Like what?"

"Let's break something. Something loud."

"Hmm, loud? Like a window?"

Ellie clapped her hands and grinned at Alfred. "A window. Perfect."

The plate glass window that overlooked the lake in the main lodge made a joyous crash as Ellie hurled a rock through it. Glass tinkled in the night. The vandals were safely hidden in the trees by the time Mr. Scanlon and Miss DeAngelo appeared from different directions. Even with her hair in curlers, the girls' gym teacher looked formidable. The beam of her flashlight searched for a culprit, but there was none to be found.

"Harriet, go back to bed," Mr. Scanlon said. "We'll deal with this in the morning."

Alfred and Ellie lay on the soft ferns under a stand of evergreens, smothering their giggles until all was silent.

Alfred turned to Ellie. "I have something to ask you. I know we haven't known each other very long, but I want you to be one of the leaders in my club."

"What?"

"Look, Bella and Tyler are getting too old. They're already starting to forget how to have fun. It's not something I enjoy doing, but they'll have to be retired. Davy is ready to take over on the boy's side and I think you'd make a great choice to replace Bella."

"Alfred, I don't know. I..." Ellie's fears for Bella were washed away by the boy's calming voice. She stared deep into his dark eyes.

"Uh oh!" He said, looking to the counselor's lodge. "I was afraid they'd pull this."

"Huh?"

"It's a spot bed check. Get back to your lodge now!"

Ellie sprinted to her lodge and made it into bed — fully clothed — without waking her bunkmates. She had time to take a deep breath, close her eyes, and relax before the door swung open and a flashlight beam swept over the bunks. When she finally heard the door close, Ellie exhaled with a whoosh. She was sweating and her heart racing, but she'd gotten away with it!

The pranks continued through July and into August. Some were silly, like dressing the Indian statue at the camp entrance in Miss DeAngelo's bra and panties. Some were gross, like a dead squirrel dangling from a miniature hangman's noose above the serving line in the mess hall. But the big hit of the summer was the *Manasquam Ghost*.

The *Ghost* was a series of one-page mimeographed newsletters, supposedly written by the spirit of the long-dead Indian chief who haunted Devil's Gulch. He savagely mocked the white invaders and threatened revenge on the campers. Though it appeared at irregular intervals, the newsletter was always eagerly scooped up. Even the staff were anxious to find out who was making goo-goo eyes at whom, who wet the bed, who cheated to pass their orienteering test. The writer's "column" was always the hit of the paper. There, the Indian chief described the tortures he would visit on the unsuspecting campers he planned to abduct. He offered clues to the identities of his planned victims, which brought the campers together trying to solve the riddle.

No one really believed the threats, but the boys loved it and the girls enjoyed shuddering in mock horror. The mid-August issue even gave the date he would make his move, August twenty-first, two days before camp ended.

By this time, Ellie had been drawn deeply into the operation of the club. In addition to enthusiastic participation in the operations, as Alfred called them, she and Bella had become the primary typists for *The Ghost*.

Ellie stuck out her tongue, concentrating as she worked on a stencil for the last issue of the newsletter. Bella sat by her side, arranging and rewriting the remaining news items.

"Do you believe it?" Bella said. "Tommy Fraser is still wetting the bed. And he's in the top bunk! Poor Donny Griffin."

"There, I got the whole paragraph done without a mistake." Ellie dropped her hands to her lap. "I wish these stupid stencils were easier to correct."

"And we both wish we were better typists," Bella laughed.

Ellie laughed too, but then turned serious. "Sometimes I feel bad about this."

"Why?"

"Don't you think some of the things we do are cruel? Poor Tommy Fraser is going to be teased by everyone at camp now. They'll call him Tinkling Tommy."

"But that's funny." Bella giggled. "Better than *Farting Fiona* in

Goose Lodge, or the *Gas Lodge* as they call it." The two girls convulsed with laughter.

When Bella caught her breath, she continued. "It's what we do. Like Alfred says, we need to have fun before we grow up and die. If Tommy and Fiona don't like being teased, then they should stop what they're doing. There are worse things than being teased."

Abduction day arrived. While everyone acted like the Old Indian's threats were a joke, many were checking to see if anyone was missing. A wave of whispers and frightened looks rolled through the mess hall. Someone was missing.

The counselors scurried among tables, anxiously checking off names on their clipboards. Relieved looks crossed the faces of each one as they found their last camper — including one boy dragged by the arm from the bathroom, red-faced and holding his shorts up with his offhand.

After finishing their checklists, each of the counselors joined in a cluster blocking the doors to the hall. In the end, there was only one CIT left frantically searching the room. Mr. Scanlon summoned him over. After a quiet but intense discussion, the camp director stepped forward.

"Campers, we're going to conduct a complete roll call. When your name is called, please rise, call out 'present' and join your lodge chief."

Slowly the names of the campers were called out and the kids wove among the tables to join their lodge mates.

"Tyler Schmidt!" There was no answer. "Tyler Schmidt, Eagle Lodge." The CIT's voice rose in both pitch and volume. "Tyler Schmidt, sound off!" Silence.

Mr. Scanlon waved the CIT over, grabbed the clipboard, and barked several questions to the boy. The director's challenging tone and the high-pitched whiny answers made the essence of the conversation clear to everyone.

Mr. Scanlon's face flushed redder as he questioned the hapless CIT. "Campers," he bellowed. "I have reached an end of my patience with this prank — in fact, all of the nasty pranks we experienced this season. Until further notice, you will stay in your lodge under the direct observation of you chief. Chiefs, escort your charges to your lodges immediately." There were a few moans about unfinished breakfasts, which Scanlon silenced with a glare.

Alfred called the club to a midnight meeting at the farmhouse. The night was filled with the sounds of peepers and crickets as Ellie and Bella followed the path through the trees. When they reached the old farmhouse all the windows were dark, but a warm yellow light streamed from the opened barn doors.

Bella stopped short, staring at the barn. "So, it's tonight," she breathed.

"What's wrong?" Ellie whispered.

Bella tried to smile through her grimace. "It's nothing. Let's go on in with the others."

The two girls stepped through the door into the glow of a hundred candles. A boy just inside the door handed each girl a sawn-off broomstick painted a deep scarlet. "Your wands, ladies," the boy said, with a bow.

Ellie followed Bella to join the other club members sitting in a circle. At its center, a cluster of candles were melted onto a deer skull, complete with antlers. Ellie's eyes flicked from the grotesque candelabra to the other members. Each held a "wand" — red for girls and black for boys.

"Bella, what's going on?" Ellie kept her voice low. The younger girl looked around to find a way out... "The boys just closed the door!"

Before she could question anything more, Alfred appeared at the edge of the circle carrying a broadsword with an ornate brass hilt. He faced outward. "From the east, we take the intellect of air."

He walked clockwise, slowly scribing a line enclosing the sitting club members. "From the south, we take the energy of fire."

Stopping at the west to invoke the intuition of water and the north for the gift of strength, Alfred completed the circle by returning to the east. He laid the sword before the deer skull and took up his wand, an axe handle painted gold with black and red stripes. His eyes travelled around the circle. "We reject the weakness, disease, and despair of adulthood. Two members have begun to grow up and must retire. We will mark their departure from our number." Alfred twirled his wand over his head and slashed down with it pointed at Bella. "Bella, step forward."

Bella rose to stand before Alfred, eyes downcast, hands folded in in front of her. Alfred raised his wand. "You've been a good playmate. Now I must lay the blessing upon you as has been done for year upon year, back to the beginning."

Bella raised her chin to look straight into Alfred's eyes. "I'm ready."

He gently touched her forehead with his wand. "You will never grow older." Each club member, in turn, stepped up to the girl, touched her forehead with their wands and repeated, "You will never grow older."

When everyone had added his or her power to the blessing, including Ellie, Alfred escorted Bella back to her place in the circle. "You may stay and revel with us until camp is done. After that, you must choose your own fate."

Alfred resumed his position in the center. Whirling and slashing with his wand, he stopped, pointing at Tyler. "Tyler, step forward."

"No, Alfred. I'm not that old. You've made a mistake." His eyes sought support among the other members but found none.

"Tyler, step forward." Alfred's voice took a harsh tone.

Tyler rose and walked to Alfred. "Alfred, you know me. There's no need for this yet," the fat boy pleaded.

Alfred raised his wand. "You've been useful. Now I must lay the blessing upon you as has been done for year upon year, back to the beginning."

There was silence while Alfred waited for an indication of acceptance from Tyler. Hearing none, he continued the ceremony. Instead of a gentle touch, Alfred brought the axe handle down on Tyler's head with all his strength. The crunching thud was the only sound for a moment. "You will never grow older."

Tyler wobbled, blood streaking down his face. He turned to Alfred, "You didn't..."

One of the bigger boys bellowed, "You will never grow older," and swung his wand, cracking it against Tyler's head, just over the ear. Tyler fell to his knees.

"You will never grow older." A blow to the face sent blood spurting. One by one the members delivered savage blows to Tyler's head and body — even the smallest kids grinned as they smashed their wands down on the moaning boy. "You will never grow older."

Bella and Ellie held back. They were now the only remaining members to not have struck Tyler's mangled form. Alfred pointed with the bloody end of his wand. "You must." Bella stood straight and defiant for a moment before slumping into acceptance. She marched forward, glaring at Alfred.

"You must," was all he said.

The girl turned and struck the lumpish mass at her feet, so hard she broke her wand. A pointed shard poked up and out of the body. For an instant, she stared at that sharp spike.

"No, Bella. Not that way." Alfred waved her back to her place in the circle, turning his gaze to Ellie.

Standing alone, Ellie pleaded, "Alfred, I don't..."

"You must." He stepped toward her. "You will be the new Red Queen. You'll succeed Bella. I have chosen it. You must."

At his touch, the thrill of power, the liquor of freedom from all rules surged through her. "You will never grow older." Her wand struck something hard in what was left of Tyler. She was thrilled by the vibrations that tingled up her arm.

Alfred laid down his wand and picked up the sword at the center of the circle. Drawing the sharp edge across his palm, he watched the blood flow for a moment before handing the sword to Ellie. The long weapon was heavy and Ellie stumbled forward, grasping the blade with both hands. She gripped it tighter until she felt it slice into the skin of her palm. As the blood dripped between her fingers, she felt the tide of dark power rise within her.

Alfred raised his bleeding palm to her. Ellie pressed her palm to his, mixing their blood.

Overflowing with a raw energy she had never known, Ellie now saw all of Alfred's limitations, his pettiness, his cruelty, his sorrows, and the source of all his power. He had imposed a terrible tradition upon the club. Her heart sang knowing that it didn't have to be so. Like a stroke of lightening, the razor-sharp sword in Ellie's hands flashed through the air neatly removing Alfred's head. It thudded to the floor and rolled to Bella's feet.

Alfred's spurting body crumpled to the floor.

Ellie's hard stare swept the circle daring anyone to step forward and challenge her. The shocked conversations fell silent. She knelt by the lifeless head of Alfred, his eyes still wide with terror. With her free hand she reached into the open gore of his throat. She burrowed her hand deep into the open wound, removing a dark stone smeared with blood and sputum.

"Now I have your devil's tongue," she hissed. She placed the stone in her mouth, dragging her slimy fingers down her face, smearing her chin with blood.

The club stared on in horror as Ellie gathered Alfred's head and hoisted it into the air. She stood and raised her bloody sword toward the heavens. "I do what I will," she shouted. "I am the Red Queen!"

27

BETTER LEFT ALONE: PART 8

"The camp was the only place we ever found bodies," Sheriff LeBuff said, dusting cookie crumbs from the front of his shirt. "Nearly two dozen of them buried in shallow graves behind some old farmhouse. The bodies were mutilated, but they hadn't decomposed. I thought it was the big break I'd been looking for before the feds swooped in and shut me down. God only knows what they did with those kids' bodies. A lot of people moved out of town after that."

Deputy LeBlanc leaned forward over his pointy knees. "What about the bikes outside?"

"They belong to the McHenry kids — Isaac, Charlie, and Logan. If they went inside the spring house, they're gone," LeBuff said. "A couple of kids disappear into that death trap every year."

"But I went into the spring house. There was nothing in there," LeBlanc said, looking at his superior officer curiously.

"Yeah, I know. I've been in there too. Many times," LeBuff turned to Anna. "We'll have to issue another search warrant."

"Yes, of course," she answered.

"How long have you lived here?" LeBlanc asked. "Are you a Campbell?"

"Well isn't he precocious?" Anna said, turning to the sheriff.

"He's diligent," LeBuff huffed. "Just answer his questions."

"But we've been over this all before. How many times..."

"Silence!" LeBuff stood and glared at Anna. "Just let him do his job."

"As you like," she said, nodding politely. She waited for the sheriff to return to his seat. Once LeBuff had settled down, Anna turned to his deputy. "I am not a Campbell," she said. "I've already told you my name. Many times."

"Watch it," the sheriff pointed.

Anna rolled her eyes. "No one around here has carried that name for a long time. I am, however, a descendant of the Campbell family, a Kirksguard. While the men may be the ones to carry the family name, it has always been the women of our family that have carried its burden. We are the ones who birth the strange boys, nurture, and love them. They are the ones cursed with the gift, and who we must watch over with a careful eye. It's not true of them all, but many of them come into this world with brilliant and troubled minds. They know things they never should know. Can do things that no one should ever be able to do. They can conceive and breathe into this world ideas that are beyond our comprehension. But this deal with the devil comes at a high price. Their gifts are sought after. They have been manipulated, prodded, and persecuted by the powerful since the beginning of time. Often they are fragile. I pity them really, all alone in this world without equal."

LeBlanc sat back into the loveseat, processing the information. "Have you always lived here?" he asked.

"No. I was raised in Kirksland, by the old quarry. I've lived in this home for just under a year. It was left in my care by an anonymous relative. To be honest, I didn't even want it. No one would buy it, so I moved in. It is quiet and pretty out here though."

"Have you ever witnessed anyone go missing?"

"Only once."

"Who?"

"Rufus White and Monica LeBuff."

"When?"

"1979."

"What did you see?"

"We were coming home from a camping trip at Devil's Gulch," Anna watched LeBuff closely. "We stopped at a burger stand along I-29 on our way..." His knuckles whitened as his fingers squeezed into the fabric of the armrest. "Gerald! Why do you keep doing this to yourself?"

Deputy LeBlanc looked to his senior officer. The sheriff was breathing heavy, his face red. "I'm sorry," LeBlanc said, changing his line of questioning. "Have you always lived here?"

"No. Shortly after my two friends disappeared, I left. Teddy and I were much maligned. People around town like Gerald LeBuff seemed to think we had something to do with the disappearances."

Anna stood and brushed the front of her dress. Sheriff LeBuff watched her carefully as she walked towards the window. She stared out into her front yard. "But that wasn't the only reason I left."

Anna turned back to face the officers and forced a smile. "I was also pregnant," she sighed. "So, I moved to Ohio to live with my aunt and uncle. Promising myself I'd never come back to this place. But here I am," she shrugged, clasping her hands. "Would either of you boys like a drink of water?"

"No thank you ma'am," LeBlanc looked at the bitter expression on the sheriff's face. "So, why did you come back here again?"

"Yeah, why did you come back here?"

"Well," Anna said, walking back to the window. "I had my reasons. Plenty of them. I resisted each opportunity," she turned back to face them again. "It wasn't until my son, Kenny, disappeared. My little buttercup. Thirteen years old. Just starting to blossom. Once he was gone, I just couldn't. I just couldn't even breathe. I couldn't even walk into my own home."

"Oh, you poor thing," the sheriff scoffed.

"Why must you always mock me?" Anna screamed. "I've been nothing but a help to you ever since I came back!"

Deputy LeBlanc leaned back and watched as Sheriff LeBuff stood and began to yell.

"What do you expect? I'm the one that's gotta go talk to the parents. Did you even bother looking outside? One of 'em was young. Real young. All three of 'em, a sister and two brothers. Gone forever, Anna! What am I supposed to think? You move back to town after not showing your face for fourteen years. You open a little inconspicuous book shop, and lo and behold, kids just start disappearing at your doorstep. How many is it now? Huh? How many?"

Anna burst into tears. "You know what your problem is Gerald? All you ever think about is yourself," she slumped into the chair and covered her face. "I have lost everyone. Everything. My father threw himself into the quarry when I was three years old. My brother hung himself in the attic of our home before it crumbled to dust. I didn't come back then. Not even to comfort my own mother. I held fast and kept my son as safe and far from this wretched place for as long as I could. I didn't even come home for my mother's funeral. She was a kind, sweet woman. Did her best. Like I've done. My poor boy. A runaway. Gone now twenty-six years."

Anna steadied herself rocking back and forth in her chair and taking deep breaths, "You act like you're the only one who's ever lost someone. I've lost my entire family. Every one of them. Why do you keep doing this, Gerald? Putting us through this? Nothing changes. You just keep trying the same thing, over and over again."

Sheriff LeBuff looked at his deputy, silver eyes stabbing his conscience. He reached into his pocket and found the stone with his fingers. He took it between his pointer and thumb, rubbing its smooth face.

"All you care about is the missing kids. You never consider the cause," Anna continued shouting. "The who, the when, the where, the how, and the why. Maybe you need to start thinking about the what? What does it want? What is it looking for?"

28

LOST STATION

op Secret: This is a secure and time sensitive document that will be automatically deleted ten minutes after opening. Please read quickly and carefully. Enclosed are highly sensitive matters of national security.

The enclosed document details our ongoing investigation into the loss of the Abyss B-23 sub-lab.

All contact was lost with Abyss B-23 on the evening of September 9. The next morning the vessel's homing beacon was identified by Naval Command and the Whale Shark submersible team was deployed from Houston. The divers were able to locate the wreckage. There were no survivors.

Though grainy, sonar dive recordings clearly show a large debris field, approximately half a mile in circumference. Most of the identifiable wreckage is comprised of large fragments of the titanium hull. The arrangement of the debris field is documented below:

Zone 1: Epicenter — little to no debris; Zone 2: Proximal — heaviest and largest debris, including hull fragments as large as 120 cubic feet and the nuclear core; the rings continue outward to Zone 5: Distal — lightest and smallest debris, including hull fragments of two cubic feet and smaller.

The pattern of the debris field suggests an internal explosion. The cause of this event is unclear and remains under investigation.

The remains of all twelve W88 warheads were found within Zones 3 and 4 of the debris field. Although the warheads were compromised, a catastrophic event appears to have been avoided.

Sea water radiation levels were recorded to be as high as 6,000 mSv at the epicenter of Zone 1 by the Whale Shark team.

All three dive team members have been hospitalized for radiation exposure.

Chances of survival: moderate.

Implications for local marine life: lethal.

NOAA data suggest that deep water radiation levels are diffusing rapidly. The highest concentrations of radiation have abated. Gulf Coast inhabitants are not believed to be at risk of overexposure at this time. No uranium recovery program is currently under consideration.

Some of the auto-luminous casings of the B-23 proved resilient in these most heinous of conditions. Both the beacon and the computer drive were undamaged and easily recovered in Zone 5 of the debris field. This small success appears to be due to the compact size of these casing models. The larger casings, used to store all forty-nine units of Formula 476/1200 D, were compromised. Only four units of the formula were used during the final phase of Operation Mephistophelian. None of the remaining forty-five units were recovered.

Implications: Uncertain.

Outlook: Moderately Optimistic.

Formula concentration rates are presumed to have diffused rapidly, diluting its strength and effectiveness. Hopes are that the radiation levels kill all marine life that might have been affected by the formula.

Of the deceased 240 crew members, notable casualties include:

Captain Eugene Elderberry: Chair of the Nautical Security Counsel of the DOD. Chair of the Office of Naval Intelligence.

General Paris Forte, First Class: DOD board member and counsel to: Office of the Director of National Intelligence, CIA, DIA, INR, and NSA.

Doctor Yuji Qian: Chief Scientist NeuroKinetics Laboratories. Dual doctorate in neurocybernetics and information systems from MIT and Harvard respectively. Leading researcher and Chief Operator of NSA Operation Mephistophelian.

Subject I-29: Declassified for these purposes only. Formerly known as Officer Kenneth Kirksguard: a decorated Green Beret and celebrated special agent of the CIA. After being infected with Russian neurotoxin Siberian Silver during a covert operation on the Crimean Peninsula, Officer Kirksguard volunteered as a subject for Operation Mephistophelian.

Unlike other subjects who rejected Formula 476/1200 D, Subject I-29's exposure to Siberian Silver appeared to provide a pathway for the neurological redevelopment and growth desired by Dr. Qian. After a brief period of observation and testing at Los Alamos, Subject I-29 was moved to the Abyss B-23 sub-lab to begin Beta phase processing.

Although Siberian Silver continued to be used as a base for Formula 476/1200 D, no other subjects have survived the Delta phase. Though anomalous, Subject I-29's continued development and survival has been credited to his inborn vitality and unbreakable spirit. As such, he remained at the Abyss B-23 sub-lab as the primary subject for Operation Mephistophelian.

Formula 476/1200 D's effects on nervous system tissue development are noteworthy. During Subject I-29's ascension through the various phases of Operation Mephistophelian his appearance underwent a multitude of changes. The continued growth of Subject I-29's nervous system diverted blood from his muscles and extreme atrophy of those structures set in immediately. Once stout and athletically built, Subject I-29 was reduced to a gaunt pallid figure with gray skin. His appendages (arms, legs, and neck) took on the appearance of taut bundled wires. The paper-thin skin that sagged from these structures tore in places, exposing pulsating blue neurons flashing with synaptic energy. His extremities (hands and feet) withered, curled and calcified into unusable stubs. He was bedridden from Delta phase on.

Multiple cranial surgeries were necessary to allow for the extensive growth of his brain. His frontal lobe protruded from the top of his head, a bulbous, convoluted, blue mass open to the air and encased in a visible electromagnetic field that buzzed noisily about him. Below that his facial structure collapsed, down to the bone. Deep in their sockets, his eyes burned, flickering yellow orbs of light. From where his nose once was, a permanent ventilation mask was installed. His heart murmured wanly in his collapsed ribcage powered by ventricular assistance devices. He received all nutrition via feeding tube and IV.

The morbid, inhuman appearance that Subject I-29 took on did not, however, speak for his incredible advancement. During the Zeta phase, when the muscles of his neck gave way and his voice box failed, Subject I-29 continued to be able to communicate with Dr. Qian and the other staff with his mind. He developed the ability to both communicate using his thoughts and to hear the thoughts of others, becoming the first known man to ever achieve verifiable telepathy.

During the Lambda phase these powers grew exponentially. He developed the ability to levitate, returning his mobility in a limited way given the machinery necessary to keep him alive. He also began interfacing with electronics using telekinesis at this time.

Continued administration of Formula 476/1200 D and surgically implanted cybernetic receptors by Dr. Qian and his team continued to amplify Subject I-29's capabilities. During Rho phase, he finally achieved bioenergetic stasis and no longer needed the aid of continued life-support. The ventilation mask was removed, and his jawbone fell away, exposing the sinuous tangle of flashing nervous tissue that now held his head upright. He could control the thoughts and actions of others. He could interact seamlessly with information systems. The yellow orbs of his eyes streamed with endless columns of binary code.

Subject I-29's ability to now override the Abyss B-23's computer system and instantaneously launch a nuclear strike made him a leading international security risk. Operation Mephistophelian was taken offline.

Internal algorithmic models produced probability outcomes far below the catastrophe standards required to continue Operation Mephistophelian.

A barrage of double-blinded psychological and behavioral tests were performed on Subject I-29 at this time. The results of all tests were positive.

Due to continued pressure from the intelligence and defense communities, the Sigma phase of Operation Mephistophelian was greenlighted.

Subject I-29 became the analytical and strategic hub for international commerce, defense, and intelligence strategies as Operation Mephistophelian continued towards its apex. It was during the Omega phase, NeoGenesis, where Subject I-29's consciousness was to converge with the World Wide Web, that the Abyss B-23 sub-lab was lost.

Although presumed deceased, Subject I-29 remains an entity of interest.

The computer drive recovered from the wreckage of the sub-lab provided a detailed cache of internal data, diagnostics, systems, logs, etc. These items have been scoured over in the hopes of identifying the cause of the Abyss B-23's destruction. No data supports a clear reason for failure. The readings show no anomalies. The sub-lab was not attacked. No system failure of any kind occurred. There is no evidence of negligence or human error. The nuclear core did not misfire. There was no earthquake or volcanic activity. No act of god, no cyber espionage, no counterintelligence, no evidence of any kind exists to suggest a reason as to why the Abyss B-23 sub-lab was lost.

None, except for a strange event captured on the surveillance video log.

The video log is filled with the full recordings from all forty-eight live action cameras that were aboard the Abyss B-23. The cameras captured every inch of enclosed space aboard the sub-lab at all times.

All duties, programs, meetings, and meals were recorded, even when the crew members slept and used the latrine. Much of this evidence is of little value. The behaviors shown align perfectly with all logs and schedules. The last few hours of footage however, although inconclusive, show an unprecedented scene.

Watching all forty-eight feeds at once it seems that nothing is out of the ordinary. The crew member rotations are as scheduled, some sleep, some are in the cafeteria — eating, chatting, or playing cards. The main deck is manned for full operation with Captain Elderberry at command, Dr. Qian and his team are convening in the control room with General Forte. All of the magnetic doors are sealed. Subject I-29 floats in the center of the fusion chamber, his heavy head tilted downwards as his body pulsates with light and electrostatic energy.

All are prepared for activation of Omega phase. The orders are given. The nuclear core is ramped to maximal output. All ancillary stations and substations are powered down as the energy from the nuclear core is directed to the fusion chamber.

The scene remains unchanged in all areas except the fusion chamber. The reflector panels turn, focusing in on Subject I-29 at the center of the room as light begins to pour in from the floor. The video feed swells with bright light, growing in intensity with each moment. Subject I-29's dark, wraithlike silhouette flutters in the radiation at the center of the screen. He floats there without moving before throwing his head back. Light appears to shoot from his eye sockets and his jawless mouth. His arms stretch wide to his sides as he leans back into the nuclear furnace of light. Slowly, his dark silhouette begins to dissipate, as if it were made of sand and blown away by the wind.

It is at this moment that the anomaly begins. Watching all forty-eight feeds at once shows that the event is synchronized. At the bottom of each video screen a wave of interference begins to bubble upwards. At the same time a subtle static sound begins to rise in volume from the microphones. All at once every crew member place their hands on their ears. Those sleeping sit up in their beds, cupping the sides of their heads. They scream in unison, slumping forward and dropping to their knees. Subject I-29 is no longer visible in the bright burning light of his feed.

The screams rise to a crescendo, garbled and high pitched. Slowly the voices are drowned out by the static as the interference continues to rise up from the base of the feeds, sloshing from side to side like water as it rises and rises, in concert with the hissing static. The screams are no longer audible, every video feed now filled with squiggled monochromatic lines of interference.

Those are the final images of all crew members aboard the Abyss B-23 sub-lab, never to be seen again. But the video feeds don't cut out, they stay live for another ninety-nine minutes. A knocking sound begins at this point, at continuous intervals, every two seconds.

Knock.

Knock.

Knock.

Then, in the distance, what sounds like a crude horn being blown can be heard intermittently as the knocking continues.

Beneath those sounds and the continued hissing of the static, in a very low and almost indiscernible register, a voice begins to speak in a deep, whispered, and aethereal tone. It repeats itself over and over again as the static, the knocking, and the horn continue.

After isolating the voice, algorithms were run in the hopes of identifying it or its origins. Our findings show that the voice, or whatever it is, appears to be speaking in a language of Chinese descent; an ancient and dead language from the Western Xia region during the Song Dynasty that predates the Mongol Invasion and the proceeding Yuan Dynasty.

If our findings are correct, the primary translation appears to be, *I'm coming. I'm coming,* repeated over and over again.

But, there is another possible translation that infers the message should be interpreted as, *I'm here. I'm here. I'm here.*

29

BETTER LEFT ALONE: PART 9

The basement of the Rustle County Police Department is rarely seen. The heavy door to the stairwell is always locked. Only one man has the key. The stairwell is lit by a single overhead bulb. Down at the bottom of the winding concrete staircase, with its metal handrails and musty damp scents, is another locked door, leading to a darkened hall. There are no lights in the basement of the police station, no windows. At the end of the hallway Sheriff LeBuff leans against the cold steel door of the storage vault. He punches the combination in on the digital keypad.

A series of gears begin to rotate as the mechanism spins and clicks behind the door. Hydraulic pistons hiss, slide free, and unlatch. LeBuff uses all his heft to push and drag the heavy metal door open on its hinges. Flashlight in hand, he walks into the vault.

The sidewalls are lined with shelving, filled with miscellaneous objects and evidence Sheriff LeBuff has gathered during his career, that Deputy LeBlanc now gathers on his behalf. There's a series of old china dolls with glass eyes of black, scrolls of parchment, old photo albums, diaries and journals, blueprints, a baseball glove, a game console, tiny fragments of black stone, all of it bagged and dated.

Sheriff LeBuff places an old forty-five record with a red 'x' slashed across its front on one of the shelves. He looks around at the bounty of his long career and sighs. He walks to the back of the vault where a series of filing cabinets and a computer wait for him. He sits down and looks at the monitor. Live feeds of digital cameras he's set up all over town show on the screen.

From his seat he watches in real time what is happening all across the county: outside of the schools, the campgrounds at Devil's Gulch, the intersection of State and Main, every strategic point and turn along Interstate 29, even the comings and goings at Belmont Asylum.

The sheriff clicks on one of the feeds. An overhead view of the main floor of the police station maximizes on the screen. He leans back in his chair and watches as Deputy LeBlanc works at his desk.

. . .

Sheriff LeBuff closes and locks the door to the basement stairs. He exits the men's bathroom, into the hall, and pushes through the swinging door into the open office space of the ground floor. Deputy LeBlanc is still sitting at his desk, working in earnest, his eyes narrowed and focused. The sheriff walks up behind his deputy and looks over his shoulder.

A map of Rustle County is spread across Deputy LeBlanc's desk. The deputy has marked points of interest across the map and is connecting the dots with a pen. He connects the final two points. The image is one Sheriff LeBuff recognizes. He's seen it before, many times. It's an enneagram, its central image a nine-pointed star. Each pair of points creates a distinct line. The network of interconnected vertices forms a perfect geometrical pattern. The image pulsates with energy.

Deputy LeBlanc points to the center of the nine-pointed star — Tower Hill. He looks up at his senior officer and smiles, "I think I'm getting close."

"Good job, LeBlanc," the sheriff says, placing his hand on the deputy's back. LeBuff looks into LeBlanc's silver eyes, his fingers searching for the circular notch between the deputy's shoulder blades.

"You're a good boy," LeBuff says, pressing the button.

Deputy LeBlanc's eyes widen slightly before going black. The deputy's head drops in lull. He slumps forward and sits motionless in his chair.

Sheriff LeBuff circles the deputy's desk and pulls the map from beneath his idle arms. "Same as last time," he says to himself, crumpling the map and throwing it in the wastebasket.

The sheriff walks over to the bookshelf and pulls one of the worn hardcovers. A hidden compartment pops free at his feet. He reaches into it and lifts a heavy toolbox from the floor. He drags the toolbox over to LeBlanc's desk and pulls up a chair behind his slackened deputy.

The sheriff searches for a flap at the base of LeBlanc's skull. Finding it, he peels the skin away revealing wires, circuits, and nodes.

"You're getting too close again," he says, opening his toolbox. He sets up his workstation, plugging an oscilloscope into the back of LeBlanc's head and powering up his soldering station.

"I can't have them coming in here and shutting me down." The sheriff puts on his safety glasses and begins to work. "It's time to start all over again."

ABOUT THE AUTHORS

Contributing Authors:

Andrea Fenton: Into the Dark, Cyborg One, and Dancing with the Dead.

Andrea Fenton writes science fiction and fantasy. She's been published in the *Shoofly* literary magazine and the Philadelphia *Inquirer*. In addition to her love of writing while drinking way too much caffeine, Andrea enjoys things like food, the great outdoors, and cats. She is a total cat lady.

Hayley E. Frerichs: What to Do When the Lights Go Out and Siren Record.

Hayley E. Frerichs writes fantasy and historical fiction for young adults and children. A Penn State graduate, she has degrees in English and education. Hayley lived and taught in southern Spain last year. She loves to travel but is also content to stay at home with her sewing machine, tea kettle, and books. Hayley's glad she doesn't live in Rustle County because, like a Regency lady, she often faints. Hayley's working on getting her epic YA fantasy adventure novel published. You can keep up with her latest writing projects on her website hayleyefrerichs.com where she blogs about zero waste and other creative hobbies.

Paige Gardner: County Theater.

Paige Gardner is a lover of all things fiction. She enjoys writing novels, flash fiction, short stories, and plays. Paige grew up in a small, unassuming town outside Pittsburgh, graduated from Penn State University, and moved to Bucks County to pursue a career in the nonprofit field. When Paige is not writing, she enjoys performing on stage, volunteering with refugee youth in Philadelphia, or enjoying a drink with close friends. Her work has been featured in Pittsburgh's In Community Magazine and 42 Stories Anthology. To keep up with Paige's writing journey, and all her writing woes, you can follow her on Twitter at @JPaigeGardner.

Jessica Kaplan: Welcome to the Circus.

    Jessica Kaplan enjoys writing flash fiction pieces and short stories. She has a degree in English, and holds a graduate degree in the field of blind rehabilitation. Currently, she is studying to become a teacher of the visually impaired. When she's not writing or practicing her braille skills, her time is spent befriending neighborhood cats, smelling flowers, and running on the mule path along River Road. She lives in Bucks County, Pennsylvania.

Bruce Logan: Campbell's Quarry.

    Bruce Logan is an author of horror, comedy, and science fiction stories and screenplays. With a career spanning 35+ years as a video producer/director, Bruce has written and directed more corporate and commercial videos than he can remember! Bruce graduated from the Philadelphia College of Art (UArts), studied at Tyler School of Art in Rome, and The Art Students League in New York City. Recently he completed Spring House, a short horror film. This collaborative effort between very talented people, including writer Adam Newton, was accepted into the 2019 Local Haunts Horrorfest at the County Theater.

James P.W. Martin: A Losing Game.

    James P. W. Martin is a storyteller of many mediums and genres. With a degree in Film Production from Emerson College, he works as a video editor, crafting stories for documentaries and TV series. His self-produced short films have been showcased in film festivals across the country. He writes screenplays, satire, and reviews for The Boundary-Bending Blog, aptly named for his provoking, genre-defying style. James lives in Bucks County, Pennsylvania where you just might be lucky enough to catch him killing it at karaoke. He is excited to have his first short story published and has big plans for more short- and novel-length stories in the future.

Bob McCrillis: Endless Summers.

Bob McCrillis writes adult fiction highlighting the heroism of ordinary people swept up in the tides of social and cultural change. His short story collection, *Puckerbrush*, was awarded the gold medal by the International Review of Books. A new collection, *Peace, Love, and A '59 Plymouth*, will be introduced at the 2019 Bucks County Book Festival. He has a novel under way and is a contributor to several literary journals. Born and raised in a small town in Maine, Bob now resides in Bucks County, Pennsylvania with his beloved wife and two spoiled dogs.

Michael Veneziale: Thunderbird Lane.

Michael Veneziale is a writer, director, and artist that lives in Bucks County, PA with his wife and two children. He wrote and directed FATV – Fantastic American Television (1997-2003), which won Best of Award in Short Attention Span Theater's Video Festival, and whose skits were featured on the UK show 'Loves Like a Dog.' He wrote and produced Miracle Shopping Network (2003-2005) a tv series and feature length film with Lance Weiler, Vince Mola, Chris Hazzard, and Angelo Cataldi. He also wrote Sci-Fi and fantasy shorts 'Pets' and 'Hollis.' Michael is currently working with 'Freestyle Love Supreme...' which opened on Broadway September 13, 2019.

Scarlet Wyvern: We All Fall and The Eyelash Weaver.

Scarlet Wyvern lives in Bucks County, PA with her young son. Wyvern has had a lifelong passion for storytelling. As a small child, she would often dictate her stories to her mother until she learned to write. Today Wyvern writes mostly poetry and young adult fantasy.

Her first poetry book entitled "Massacre My Heart" is being released later this year. Wyvern attends Bucks County Community College where she is pursuing a degree in web design. Her dream is to start a game design company. A self-proclaimed nerd, Wyvern can often be found gushing over Doctor Who, Game of Thrones, and Supernatural as well as lamenting the early cancelation of Firefly. An avid fan of fantasy, Wyvern can easily be persuaded to read anything featuring dragons or magic. Wyvern is fascinated by mythology, especially that which concerns the fair folk. Wyvern is obsessed with the original Grimm fairytales. This is Wyvern's first publication.

Adam J. Newton: Into the Deep, Turn Right on Belmont Avenue, Lillie of the Field, The Weeping Song, A Paper Unicorn, The Spring House, The Lost Station and Better Left Alone Parts 1-9.

Adam J. Newton is the fearless leader and organizer of the Bucks County Writers Group. A self-proclaimed "townie," Adam grew up and has lived in Doylestown, PA for most of his life. When this jack of all trades isn't traveling the world, teaching, or writing, you will find him curled up in an armchair with a good book and his dog Minima in his lap. His screenwriting debut, Spring House, a short horror film directed by Bruce Logan, was accepted into the 2019 Local Haunts Film Festival at the County Theater. Creaky Stairs is Adam's first publication, but he promises it won't be his last. For more information about Adam go to www.thebcwritersgroup.com.

Made in the USA
Middletown, DE
29 September 2019